AMONG THE DEAD AND DREAMING

Also by Samuel Ligon

Wonderland

Drift and Swerve

Safe in Heaven Dead

AMONG THE DEAD AND DREAM-ING

SAMUEL LIGON A NOVEL

Leapfrog Press
Fredonia, New York

Published in 2016 in the United States by
Leapfrog Press LLC
PO Box 505
Fredonia, NY 14063
www.leapfrogpress.com

Printed in the United States of America

Distributed in the United States by
Consortium Book Sales and Distribution
St. Paul, Minnesota 55114
www.cbsd.com

Author photo by Heather Malcolm

First Edition

Library of Congress Cataloging-in-Publication Data

Names: Ligon, Samuel, author.
Title: Among the dead and dreaming / Samuel Ligon.
Description: First edition. | Fredonia, NY : Leapfrog Press, 2016. | St. Paul, Minnesota : Distributed in the United States by Consortium Book Sales and Distribution
Identifiers: LCCN 2015041419 (print) | LCCN 2015044192 (ebook) | ISBN 9781935248781 (softcover) | ISBN 9781935248798 (epub)
Subjects: LCSH: Single mothers--Fiction. | Man-woman relationships--Fiction. | BISAC: FICTION / Literary. | FICTION / Contemporary Women. | FICTION / Psychological. | FICTION / Romance / Gothic. | GSAFD: Romantic suspense fiction.
Classification: LCC PS3612.I35 A83 2016 (print) | LCC PS3612.I35 (ebook) | DDC 813/.6--dc23
LC record available at http://lccn.loc.gov/2015041419

For My Mother and Father

Fish die belly upward and rise to the surface.
It's their way of falling.

—André Gide

What falls away is always. And is near.

—Theodore Roethke, *The Waking*

AMONG THE DEAD AND DREAMING

1

CYNTHIA

The rain was more like mist, soft against your skin the way the air is down by the ocean, so beautiful and calm, even from the back of Kyle's motorcycle. I wanted to go faster and faster through it, my eyes closed tight and the water running off my face. It was just me and Kyle, or me and the ocean, me and the rain, or not me at all, just Kyle, the ocean, the rain, until we hit something and I was weightless, flying, the anticipation of landing lifting me into this bright, raw awareness. Nothing had been settled. Nothing ever would be settled. Nothing was supposed to be settled. And nothing was supposed to be accomplished, either, except the baby in my belly, the beautiful baby I wrapped myself around as we flew. Mark didn't know about her—I'd only been certain a few weeks myself— but I sometimes thought she might save us. I didn't know her name yet, not for sure. I just thought, baby, baby, baby, the one good thing I was going to do with myself, the one good thing I'd have. And then I did know her name for sure—Isabelle. My sweet baby Isabelle. Those moments we were in the air seemed like they might go on forever.

KYLE

The sky was pale green between purple clouds until the fog moved in and made everything gauzy. You could hardly tell the sand from the sky, and the ocean wasn't visible at all, just a rumble out in the soup somewhere. We ate our dinner and wrapped ourselves in a blanket, and even though she had Mark and I had Nikki, I didn't really have Nikki, not the way I wanted to have her, and Cynthia and Mark were unraveling again. So we'd come to the beach without them. We'd known each other for years, me and Cynthia. We'd known each other forever. When the fog turned to drizzle, we got back on the bike and headed home, Cynthia against me shouting, "Come on, faster!" One minute we're grounded in this gauzy, white mist, the next minute we're weightless, up, coming down, but I'm thinking okay, until I realize she's gone, out in the fog somewhere. Except she's not gone. I can hear her voice, "Come on, faster," like she's right up against me, even as I'm wrestling the bike through a skid, leaving skin all over the asphalt. I didn't know anything for a long time after that, didn't hear anything or want anything. I became aware of my heartbeat in my ears, muddy and monotonous, and then I was outside myself and frantic, listening as hard as I could—to paramedics shouting, to tires hissing and the sound of the ocean over the berm, to a train's whistle across South Oyster Bay. But I couldn't hear Cynthia anymore, anywhere.

NIKKI

The light in the waiting room is the same dull light, and the people coming and going have always come and gone, and his father rubs my shoulders, and his mother's face is carved by tears, and Cynthia's parents hold each other while Mark smolders, all of us underwater for what feels like forever. I try so hard to believe he's going to pull through, almost like praying, or willing the life back into him, when it's probably only Cynthia who could do that, and she died at the scene. But he keeps not pulling through. And I'm sick with myself, knowing I should have loved him more or loved him better, or just let him go, since I never could have loved him more or better. At least he had Cynthia. At least I think he did, hope he did. *Almost anyone would have been better than me*, I want to tell him, as though admitting the poverty of my love will keep him alive to hear my confession. I need him now more than I've ever needed him, and now that I need him, I won't get him, exactly what I deserve. The surgeon who finally tells us is the hairiest man I've ever seen. I know before he says a word that Kyle's dead. Everyone knows. It's in the way he carries himself, slumped toward us through the swinging doors, all the color drained from his face. I look for pieces of Kyle woven into the fur of his forearms. I watch his mouth move, Kyle's mother collapsing, all these millions of hairs reaching out of his scrubs, and all I can feel—all I've felt for weeks, really—is Burke out there waiting, a shark in deep water swimming circles toward shore. And I think, Kyle. I sit back in my seat with my face in my hands, trying to hold on to him, the whisper of his breath and the heat coming off his skin, how we'd dance sometimes while dinner was cooking, when the light was just right and the wine was just right and the music was perfect, everything we had and might have had here now with me.

MARK

Her father's voice on the phone was like an infection, my throat catching and closing as I sat trying to calm down, not wanting to calm down, holding onto the loss of her. I didn't know she died with Kyle, so for a few minutes my grief was all there was—until

I got to the hospital and found out they crashed together, bringing on this panic of love and loss and tiny, black-hearted hatred. I couldn't stand to think of her gone from me, gone with him. I couldn't stand to think of the world without her. But in the dead air of the waiting room, her presence was everywhere, and then her absence, and then her presence again, so that her presence and absence felt like the same thing. I could smell something that smelled like her, or I could hear—something—a whisper or hum, her voice—somewhere. My breath was too shallow, stuck in my chest, and I heard her whisper, "Breathe," but when I took a deep breath and held it, not breathing, she didn't say anything. Nobody did. Everyone was crying and pacing and disappearing and reappearing. No one could comfort anyone else. After Kyle was pronounced dead, Nikki put her face in her hands for a long time. I touched her shoulder and she looked at me with her eyes shot and her face broken, and then she covered up again. I drove to Cynthia's place under a weak blue sky, the sun still rising behind me. I couldn't think of any other place to be.

ISABELLE

Oh.

2

Nikki

At seventeen, I ran from home with a boy named George who left me broke on the street in Providence. I never found another love like we had those weeks before he disappeared, though I looked for it everywhere I went. That was my real problem, all that searching and hunger. I didn't know you can only fall in love and run from your mother once in your life. George was the best mistake I ever made.

I stayed in Providence for months after he left, then moved to Austin, where I met my worst mistake—Cash. Maybe I was too hungry, remembering my time with George, or maybe we got together too fast, before I could really know him, but whatever the reason, pretty soon it was just me and Cash and nothing else in the world that mattered. We were happy, too, until I started looking for work. He had plenty of money, he told me, would buy me whatever I wanted. What I wanted, I told him, was my own money. I got a job at a barbecue place and the interrogations started. I wasn't interested in anyone else, but he'd accuse me of cheating or plotting to cheat. Why else would I talk to someone or look at someone or go to a coffee shop or have ever been born?

I'd been independent too long to put up with that kind of shit. But I did put up with it—until he called me *mouthy*.

"What did you say?" I said, and he said, "I'm tired of the mouth on you," and I said, "So leave," and he said, "I don't want to leave," and we got into it worse than ever before, fighting all night.

He said it again a week later—"What'd I say about *mouthy?*"— and that's when I knew it was over for good. But he promised to change, and even though I knew better, I forgave him. We lived in a big house on Duval Street, with a lot of other people, him in the basement, and me on the second floor. After I took him back, he started spying on me. "You don't know what love is," he told me, before and after I broke it off for good. "You don't know what love is," he told me as he stalked me and haunted me for months.

He'd break into my room, follow me around, and the more cold and pissed off I became, the more threatening he became, unhinged and dangerous, until I finally had to move out of that house. But I didn't run far enough—only across town, where I thought I was hidden. There was a moment of rest then, maybe a month. I was so young and stupid, so hungry for love, even after all that. Maybe *because* of all that. I fell for this guy, Daryl, and Cash tracked me down and hurt me more than I'd ever been hurt before. I ran to Oregon, where I waited for Alina to be born, praying she was Daryl's baby, but the minute I saw her face, blood streaked and furious, I knew she'd come from Cash. She had attached earlobes like his and my eyelids, and she was the most beautiful thing I'd ever seen, even if she did come from Cash.

I never meant to kill him. Or I meant to and couldn't follow through and then he died anyway, before I ran from Austin with Alina just a speck in my belly. So Kyle wasn't my first boyfriend to die—just the one I could have made a life with, maybe, if things had been different. What happened with Cash was self defense and another reason to get on another bus and keep moving, always moving from the minute I left my mother in Manchester, always hoping to lose myself completely.

I didn't know Cash had a brother until Burke called a few

weeks ago. For a second when I heard his voice, I thought Cash was back from the dead. I couldn't make sense of the moment, because I didn't know Burke existed. The sound of his voice on the phone stripped me to something I didn't want to recognize in myself, like I was eighteen again, sprung to run, ready to pop. But I wasn't eighteen. I was thirty-one. And the only thing that mattered was making sure Burke never found out about Alina.

ALINA

My mom talks about the mistakes she made when she was young and wild, but she never tells me what I want to hear. My father, she says, died in a car accident before I was born. Other than that, she won't talk about him at all. Ever. I've never seen a picture or met a grandparent. "What about diseases and stuff?" I used to ask. "What about genes?" I knew that would get to her because of her own mother's death from cancer. And her aunt's.

"What about genes?" she said.

"I should know who he is," I said, "where I came from."

"You came from me," she said.

"You don't know his name?"

"Jim," she said.

But sometimes he had other names.

That was when we were living in Seattle, before I learned to stop asking. They skipped me a grade, from second to third, because I was bored and getting in trouble and she wouldn't let them put me on drugs. She was with Hal then, off and on, a guy she met at the restaurant. I didn't care about Hal. I didn't care about any of them until Kyle.

NIKKI

"Make sure Kyle calls *and* writes," Alina told me yesterday morning, before I left her at her new school in Michigan. "He will," I said, so grateful she was gone. Now, I'll have to bring her home and get her away again safe, but with a broken heart this time.

Months ago, I was furious with Kyle for encouraging her to attend Interlochen. He knew I couldn't afford boarding school, that I didn't want her in a place filled with rich kids, that I didn't want to lose her so young. But he kept talking about the place. He'd gone to art school himself and it changed him, he said, made him a better person. He wanted to pay her way, whatever wasn't covered by scholarships. We'd only been seeing each other a few months.

"She doesn't have to know where the money comes from," he said one night when we were watching the water from a bench on the boardwalk. "It'll be like another scholarship," he said.

Alina was at a friend's house. We hadn't talked about it in weeks.

"And if it doesn't work out, she can come home."

He looked so open and vulnerable, so hungry to help.

"I appreciate the offer," I said. "I really do," and he said, "So let me do this," and I wondered if I could—for Alina's sake, but also because I thought falling into his debt might be good for me, too, an act of faith, a kind of surrender. I didn't want to hold myself so tight forever. I surprised us both when I took him up on his offer a few days later, grateful for his help, until Burke called, and then I was just grateful for a place to hide Alina, pulling back from faith and surrender as fast as I could.

Kyle loved me, I know that much, whether I deserved it or not. But he was in love with Cynthia, too, and had been for years. She was rich like him and careless about money, careless about everything, the way rich people always are. The nudes he painted of me had her eyes, the reason I couldn't love him right, because he was in love with her, the lie I told myself, the lie I keep telling.

3

BURKE

I did fifteen years for Cash, most of them after he was killed down in Austin, and when I got out all I wanted to do was get in the Goat and go. But of course nobody'd taken care of her—the one thing I asked Cash to do—hoses rotted, radiator rusted, tires shot to hell, even though he told me he used the fuel stabilizer and put her up on blocks. But no. It was the same beer cans and dough- nut sacks and empty packs of cigarettes from 1986 scattered all over her cracked and rotting upholstery, one of the vent windows wide open. You'd think I'd have been filled with rage to see such a mess, but I was past all that, something I learned from Carl down at Huntsville—the guiding hand of fate deciding everything for a reason, so you might as well just surrender to it and become its instrument, since that's all you're ever going to be anyway.

After Cash died, that GTO was the one thing I had on the outside besides our mother, starlight black with a bobcat kit I installed myself. It was a '67 convertible I picked up over in Cor- sicana when I had more money than I knew what to do with, a year out of high school and thinking the ride would never end. Another trick Carl taught me about doing easy time was find- ing a place in your mind nobody knew about, a place you es- caped to and lived a secret life you couldn't live inside. I made the

Goat that place in my mind all them years at Huntsville—driving around with beer on ice in back, Suzy Mullins or Kate Blisdale in the bucket seat beside me wearing a yellow tube top or baby tee, a sweet powdery smell mixing with the gas and weed and beer smells inside the Goat, and Zeppelin or Skynyrd on the tape deck pushing us out to eternity.

When I got out of our mother's truck, finally home from Huntsville, the Goat's cover was shredded—hail storms, she told me—the finish flat and dull and pocked. Nothing like what I imagined all them years away. You'd think after that long inside a man would have all kinds of pent up energy ready to explode, but doing time mostly just wears you out, like years gone drunk or dreaming. Our mother was worn out too, my time away and Cash dead and gone, so that I could hardly stand to sit with her nights in front of the television, a nervous energy starting to run under the weight of all them wasted years. Even with my parole officer hounding me to get a job, start over and find a girl, I knew I had to align myself first and figure out what the guiding hand had in store for me.

I sat in the Goat most evenings, smoking and watching the sun go down. Our mother came out one night with a can of beer she knew I wasn't supposed to have and sat beside me in the dark. "There's plenty of girls who'll love a hardworking man," she told me. "Plenty of girls who can forgive the past." I got up the next morning and started circling job ads in the newspaper. That's when the anger started rising, the Goat behind our mother's house used up and the anger rising as the guiding hand found its use for me. Not that I could see it yet. Not that I could name it. But I could feel it a little, change coming like a cool wind, something shifting down in my guts guiding me toward a life I wanted to live, a sweet cool wind just beginning to blow.

CASH

Sometimes I hated her, sure, just like anyone, but mostly I loved her. I was just trying to take us back to before, and she was the one who always played that Billie Holiday song, "You Don't Know What Love Is," the words I spit back in her face later—not that it did any good. I was fucked up is all, this pressure grinding me down like I was going to explode if she didn't wake up and help take us back where we belonged. I had everything before she took it away. That ain't right—to give somebody something and then yank it away. I gave her a bracelet once, turquoise and silver, and found it broken on the floor of her room at Duval after her and Melanie ran. That pissed me off more than anything—just how easy she could throw things away, like there was never a thing between us. But I forgave her. Even though I wanted to kill her sometimes, it was only in my mind, and I forgave her, me going to her like I did that night really just a part of my forgiveness.

NIKKI

I woke not knowing or knowing it wrong, Cash in my bed, but thinking it's Daryl. Then knowing it's Cash, not Daryl. And if not Daryl, it's not what I dreamed it was of us making love, but something else. And if something else—I started to thrash. He punched me hard, cutting me with his ring. He punched me again and I pretended surrender, this roar in my ears. Because it was not Daryl, because it was something else, he should have known I would never surrender. If he knew me at all, he should have known that much.

I reached and pulled and finally grabbed the knife from my pants pocket on the floor by my bed, fumbling with it behind his back, all this hatred and fear running so hot inside me. I opened it and lifted it and brought it down hard, and after he jumped, howling, I jumped, too, ready to stab again if he should come at me, screaming at him from the top of my lungs to get out, get out! He scrambled away while I stood on my bed with the knife cocked, my heart beating through my whole body, and I never felt so powerful—until the adrenalin wore off and I didn't want to live anymore if he was alive.

But I didn't drop down to my bed like I wanted to.

I went looking for Daryl, looking for people to surround myself with. I couldn't find the right people though, so I made my way to the big house on Duval, hating Cash as hard as I could, stoking my hatred to make myself strong. Because I thought it would be him or me. Because I knew he would get a gun or a knife or just use his hands, and he'd come back for me and do it again. And he'd kill me. I didn't want to give up my life like that, but my hatred was running out, and I didn't know if I'd be able to hurt him, to kill him. I didn't think I could, even though I knew I had to.

I found him sprawled on the basement couch at Duval, barely awake on liquor and pills. I stood over him, but I didn't know what to do with myself, didn't know how to get back to myself. I'd always been strong, but that part of me seemed gone. I ran upstairs looking for something until I found a bigger knife, and then I tied him with twine—he was unconscious. I chopped off the tip of his finger, his pinky, hardly knowing myself at all. I bandaged the stub and ran, not knowing he'd bleed to death from his earlier wound, the stabbing, not knowing I'd be the one to survive.

I took his fingertip with me to Oregon, wrapped in a pink silk pouch. I still have it. I kept telling myself it doesn't count as rape if you've slept with the guy before, not half believing it even then. But I had to tell myself something. I lived off my hatred and fear for months, hunkered down like an animal as Alina came

23

to life inside me. I made myself strong for the baby, thinking of the Patti Smith lyric—"Jesus died for somebody's sins, but not mine"—and how I didn't owe anybody anything. I was all rage and impotence, impotence and rage. After Alina was born, I realized Cash had been right all those times he told me I didn't know what love was. I learned what it was loving her.

4

BURKE

Cash was still in high school when I got busted, bringing in as much money as me, maybe more—the point being, we was in it together. But when the cops crashed in, drawing down on me at six in the morning, I didn't know I was sitting on all that blow Cash had stashed to move the next day. One of the pigs brought it out from my closet, and I knew I was going to prison, thinking they'd planted it, before learning later it was Cash bringing us down. So I took the fall, same as he would have done for me, and then, maybe a year later, somebody murdered him before he could even pretend to turn himself around. That's when I started doing hard time, awful time, rotting for nothing.

I studied his murder once I got out, but that was fifteen years gone by, and nobody in Waco knew who he was running with in Austin. It was most likely wrong place, wrong time, somebody ripped off or somebody jacking him, guiding hand of fate or I didn't know what. The missing finger made me think of a Mexican gang, some payback shit I didn't know about.

Let it go, our mother said when I asked about it time and again. Let him rest.

I settled into a line cook's job at Denny's, settled into something with a girl named Connie. I don't know if we just grew tired of one another or what, but once she went back to Dallas, I had time on my hands. When a stroke killed our mother, time was the only thing I had. I thought a lot about Cash then, wishing he was home with me to go through our mother's belongings, to remember our lives together as kids, back before we could imagine everything would go to shit like it always does in the end.

I didn't know about Nikki until I found a box of Cash's stuff in my mother's closet. There was an address book in there with Nikki's name scribbled across the pages, and lots of other words he wrote about her—how she was hot one day and cold the next, how she was the only one he'd ever love, a beautiful angel, a fucking bitch, his sweet, darling baby, a dirty little whore. There was a bundle of polaroids, too, pictures of this beautiful girl—Nikki, I guessed—some of her alone and half naked, and some of her with him near the end of his life, when he wore long sideburns and a sculpted leather cowboy hat. She must've been nineteen, twenty years old, Cash looking so proud in a picture of him and her by the river—you know he couldn't half believe he got her.

I flipped through them pictures, glad for Cash to have found such a piece of ass, but wondering too why it couldn't be me that had her—right now, the living one—wondering if they killed her after they killed him, if they took her and did unspeakable things before dumping her across the border, or if they paid her off and let her go, if she betrayed him somehow, making it all the worse, because she was what he had and cared for. I wondered if they tied her down, like they tied Cash down. I wondered if she was true to him at the end, if she loved him then and forever, if she was still suffering for him to this day. I never had a girl tear at me the way she tore at him. I could tell from the pictures it was the kind of big bad love I'd only ever heard about in songs.

I knew he lived with a band down on Duval Street, in the same house they killed him at. I drove down there and found the drummer, Bo, and asked about Cash's girl, this Nikki he was so torn up over.

"You'd never forget her," Bo said, and I knew it was true, a fever starting to burn in me even then.

I showed him one of the pictures, and he said it was her, said she worked at Stubbs back then, but disappeared maybe a month before they killed Cash.

I thanked him and drove back to Waco. I sat in the Goat, night after night, looking at her pictures and wondering what had happened between the two of them. Connie wouldn't return my calls from her high horse in Dallas, so I drove up there one night and banged on her door until she threatened to call the cops. But she wasn't half as hot as that Nikki, the girl Cash had while I was rotting. It didn't seem like I'd ever be so lucky as to find a girl as good as he found in her, a girl to love and get torn up over, a girl as beautiful as that. I could tell by the way she looked at him in the pictures how bad she had it for him, how bad they had it for each other. I wondered if she was still alive, torn up over Cash, still aching for something only a Chandler man could give her.

5

ALINA

I know something's wrong by the tone of her voice, but even after she tells me Kyle's dead, I don't believe her.

It's a trick, I think. She must have learned he's coming to Interlochen Wednesday to visit.

"This is about next week," I say, "isn't it?"

"Next week?"

"You know."

But she doesn't know.

She tells me about the accident. Crying and everything.

"Okay," I say, still not believing, even though there's electricity in my hands.

"They're going to scatter his ashes in the Sound Saturday," she says.

But he's coming here Wednesday, I think.

"This woman he died with," she says. "It's crazy."

And I'm like, "What woman?"

"This girl he grew up with. Cynthia."

And I'm like, "What girl?"

She doesn't say anything then.

I swear to god, she must be in shock.

And then, for a second, it hits me. Kyle. But just as fast I don't believe. Then I do, then I don't, then I do. And I'm like, Kyle. Then nothing. My big heavy dorm phone against my face. Then Kyle. I'm crying hysterical so a part of me must know. But another part doesn't. He's coming here Wednesday to visit. Just him and me. He's dead. One thing seems to have nothing to do with the other. He's coming here Wednesday to visit.

NIKKI

I walk the beach and boardwalk for hours, a faraway line of container ships shimmering through the waves of haze and humidity. When we first moved from Seattle, Alina wanted to live down here near the ocean, but my job selling ads for the *Long Island Weekly* barely covered our bills month to month. We kept looking for a place we could afford until we found our little cottage in Long Beach, and then it seemed like nothing could ever touch us again. The best part of Alina's childhood has been here, the most stable part, and these last few months with Kyle have made her feel, I don't know, fuller maybe, part of why I wanted to build something with him—because *she* loved him so much. And after so many years, it seemed like I was ready for something, too.

A shopping cart sits on the beach, its tracks leading back to the water, as if somebody pushed it out of the ocean. I want to preserve her ignorance, buy her peace with my silence, but every second I wait to tell her feels like a betrayal.

When I finally go home and call her, she makes me say it again and again—Baby, there's been an accident. Kyle's gone. Yes. An awful accident. No. Kyle's dead. I'm sure, yes. Oh, honey. He's gone. No, I'm positive—until she finally breaks, crying and crying, and I know I should have told her in person, of course I should have. What kind of mother gives her daughter such news on the phone? I couldn't afford another ticket, though, and put off calling for far too long, hoping to never tell her, as though I could have kept her safe and away forever.

She cries and cries, and I can't touch her, can't hold her. What kind of mother?

Hours later, when I hear her sleeping across the miles, her breathing soft and even on the phone, I take Cash's finger bone from its pouch, but the finger tells me nothing. Years after he died, I felt bad for Cash—sad and sorry—just because he was responsible for Alina. I'd look at that fingertip as it rotted and became nothing but a chip of bone, all that was left of him, and feel as though I'd taken something from her. I never forgave him for what he did, but I couldn't forgive myself either. I couldn't even tell what might be forgiven in me, exactly, and what pieces of my past would always be unforgivable.

6

MARK

Cynthia's answering machine blinked four messages, but I knew not to check them, because checking them would mean she was never coming back. I wandered her place, picking things up and putting them down, smelling everything, Any second, it seemed, she'd walk through the door. "You're never going to believe what happened," she'd say, and I'd make us breakfast while she told me. There was a picture of us on her bookshelf, slouched into her parents' couch the night I met Kyle in his black leather pants, finally home from his years in Asia. They were old friends from country clubs and summer camp, Cynthia and Kyle, and I'd been changing the subject away from him for years.

I went to her room and piled clothes on her bed, armfuls from her closet and dresser drawers, underwear, sweaters, dresses, skirts. I burrowed into all of it. Whether or not she'd been sleeping with him, or for how long, hardly mattered now. I turned off the light, wanting to see her more than I had in months, to touch her and taste the salt and sweetness of her skin. Things had been bad between us since spring, but to never see her again? We always came back to each other. I picked up a sweater, smelled it, and threw it on the floor. The cat people dropped something upstairs, what sounded like a sledge hammer. I unwound a ball of

31

leather, thinking it would turn into her red leather pants, but the legs were too long for her red leather pants.

I sat up and turned on the light. The pants were black—of course they were. I rifled the pockets, finding a box of Nat Sherman Classics, Kyle's pretentious cigarettes. I could hardly breathe. The secret lovers were dead forever with their secret that wasn't secret anymore. Or maybe it was more secret now. Or maybe his clothes in her room meant nothing at all. I grabbed his cigarettes and pants and ran out of there, expecting to see her every second—running up the stairs as I ran down, calling my name from across the street once I was outside, following me home from Brooklyn on the LIE. "You're never going to believe what happened," she'd say, and there would be comforting explanations for everything.

Elizabeth

It's not that I didn't like her, I hardly even knew her, had met her only twice, when Tom and I flew to Providence to visit Mark at school. She was attractive and polite, too polite, I might have said, and she was sick that second time, Mark's senior year, so sick she could hardly drag herself out of bed. It all seemed a little showy to me, something about their obsessive, touchy behavior, their devotion to each other, that felt just a little uncouth. Tom and I had dated all kinds of people in college, discovering who we were and what we liked, but those two—attached at the hip from first semester on. And the jealousy! I was careful not to show disapproval, knowing I could push him deeper into her arms that way. I kept my own counsel, comforted myself knowing it wouldn't last, couldn't last, and when it was finally over between them, Mark came back to Chicago and started working in politics, but with good people and for real change. Those were happy years, before I got sick. He met a woman at work I thought he'd marry. Liz. She was bright and driven, a reader, a cook. She said she didn't want children, but lots of women say that. When Mark left his job with the congressman, I didn't understand why until I found out Cynthia was in New York. "What about Liz?" I asked. She was in Washington full time with the congressman then, while Mark ran the field office. Maybe the distance between them was too much. Maybe he didn't like that she was his boss, though I hoped I'd raised him better than that. In the weeks before he left he'd visit the house and sit with me, read to me. He'd bring vanilla ice cream and I'd pretended to enjoy it, though nothing appealed to me anymore. Everything tasted like metal. I couldn't beg him to stay away from her. It wouldn't do any good. I didn't believe in God, but I prayed He would help my son find the right woman to love.

MARK

I was forgetting her smell, the exact feel of her hands. The second I got home, I called her machine to study her voice. Maybe if she'd known she was going to be dead, she would have put more thought into her recorded greeting, singing or leaving instruction for the living: "Don't ride on motorcycles," she could have said, or, "Run up enormous credit card debt." Until I'd moved from the city a few months before, my aunt's place had been empty almost a year, and it still held phantom odors—old people smells mostly and decades of cigarettes. I imagined Cynthia at the table, pulling Nat Shermans from the pack and filling the kitchen with smoke.

"Now you're buying them?" I would have said.

"Kyle left them."

"His pants, too?"

"I'm not doing this," she would have said, and I would have

said, "Of course you're not," and we would have kept working that seam until we exhausted it.

I lit one of Kyle's cigarettes and noticed a picture of my mother hung by the basement door. There were pictures of her all over the house. Sometime during the long months of her illness, a shrink had told me the sick and dying live in a world the healthy can't inhabit or comprehend. We can hardly even visit. Or, if we do, we're merely tourists who need to get away fast as a matter of self-preservation. I'd just moved to New York from Chicago when my mother died, and was back with Cynthia after all those years since college. For a little while, we were able to bring something soft out in each other, a tenderness I hadn't known in years.

Then Kyle appeared, bringing our fighting and jealousy out of remission. We started arguing, like we'd argued through multiple break ups in college, the silences between our arguments growing and taking on weight. She talked about babies more as we drifted apart, an obsession I didn't understand. Why would we have children now, when we seemed more unstable every day? And if it wasn't babies, it was Kyle she talked about, until I couldn't stand to hear any of it.

"What do you think of the name Isabelle?" she asked one night. "For a little girl?"

I didn't think anything of the name Isabelle—because we weren't going to have a little girl. Not then. Not ever. We were about done it felt like.

"Kyle wants me to pose for him," she said, and I said, "Pose," and she said, "Nude," and I didn't say anything.

"Are you moving to Long Island to get away from the city," she said, "or to get away from me?"

"My aunt's house is empty," I said. "And Garden City's not far."

"You're the only person I know," she said, "who would move to the suburbs *not* to have children."

But there were good times too—plenty of them—although, toward the end, if we weren't fighting, everything felt fragile between us, like we were just waiting for the glue to take hold and wondering if it ever would.

I smoked another Nat Sherman at my aunt's kitchen table. Cynthia was going to walk through the door any second and we'd argue about Kyle's pants. We needed a catalyst, a last argument to determine if we were going to break up for good or start finding a way back to each other. It was just a matter of smoking and waiting. I hadn't seen her in weeks, since before her family reunion up at Lake George. This night was no different than any other night she'd been gone. Unless I chose to believe she was gone for good. It was hotter than hell in my aunt's kitchen. I lit another cigarette and waited.

7

CYNTHIA

Wanting her became a kind of sickness, as if I'd been infected with longing for this nameless, faceless entity who would grow in me and make herself known to me and, after she came out of me, keep growing into who she would become. I guarded against my selfishness, this wanting I felt to bring her to life, so deep in me it overwhelmed my fear of the cliché I seemed to be embracing, biological clock or whatever it was. None of that mattered. Months before I was pregnant, she existed in me, of me and separate from me too, teaching me how to transcend the enormous selfishness of this world, and then I wasn't even aware of selfishness or my want, because I'd already transcended that and was living only for her. I was far past wondering if she'd fill some hole in my life. She'd already filled it, or if there wasn't a hole, she'd already made my life so much larger—finally giving me this profound reason to live. I'd known love as a child and a sister, a lover and a friend. But this was different, deeper, so deep I could hardly believe Mark couldn't feel her everywhere around us. She was there, somewhere, I don't know how many months before I was pregnant, waiting for me, her demands on my attention the beginning of this enormous gift. All I wanted to do was find her.

NIKKI

The minute Alina sees me at LaGuardia she bursts into tears. I take her in my arms and hold her, trying to ignore the men in business suits checking us out as she cries into my shoulder. At thirteen, Alina could pass for seventeen and we could be sisters, but that thought reminds me of my mother's awful vanity and what the first mastectomy did to her, how it made her hate herself, as though her body—her beauty—was all she'd ever had. For the first time in days, I wonder when I'll get the cancer that killed her, when Alina will, and then I forget all that and the men gliding by and everything else as I breathe her in, rubbing my hands over her head, through her hair, over the soft skin at the base of her neck, my beautiful, beautiful baby.

MARK

Cynthia's parents were at the funeral home when I arrived, waiting in a room with velvety gold wallpaper and overstuffed chairs. I wasn't prepared for how much they'd aged in the hours since I'd left the hospital. They looked like they'd been awake for weeks, starving. "We're glad you're here," Denys said. "We know you want to be alone with her." I wasn't sure I wanted to be alone with her, but a man with a silver pompadour escorted me to a reception room where Cynthia's casket sat on a stand surrounded by blown up photographs—Cynthia eating birthday cake, Cynthia on a horse, Cynthia and me on her parents' patio. Seeing her up there everywhere made her seem both closer and further away, all those images evoking her, but also emphasizing her absence.

I wondered if Pompadour had seen her naked, if he'd handled her body. Of course he had. So what? From the back of the room I looked at her casket, only the top section of which was open. I walked toward her, thinking I wouldn't recognize her, but I did, and she looked . . . not good, but not as bad as I'd expected, either. Her face seemed deflated and inflated, as though bones had broken before everything collapsed and swelled, shades of purple and yellow rising through her makeup. I petted her hair. Pompadour had probably washed it for her. I didn't want to keep studying her for signs of damage.

I remembered going to the Cape spring break freshman year with a group of friends we later used as weapons—my roommate Phil, a girl named Sarah, Ben and Julie. It was Sarah's parents' summer place, and Cynthia and I were given the master bedroom. Not everyone at Brown came from money, but everyone I knew did. They weren't snotty, though, not even Cynthia, whose father's annual bonuses from Goldman Sachs were more than my father would earn in his life. Ben and Julie hooked up that trip. Phil and Sarah got married later. After five months together, Cynthia and I still could not stop touching each other. The six of us stayed up late, talking and drinking, and then Cynthia and I walked the beach for hours. We didn't need to tell each other anything then. We knew everything we needed to know and what everyone else knew, the reason we were given the master bedroom. And it seemed that now that we'd arrived at this place of fullness or perfection—love or whatever it was—we would always inhabit it, would never change or age or grow dull to each other. It was just that we were young and in love for the first time. And time itself was different then. So much more was always happening.

Standing over her body, I could hardly put the chronology together, could hardly believe we'd start our cycle of cheating and clinging only five or six months after that morning on the beach. But that was long before any hint of erosion. When we finally returned to the sleeping house, we made a big breakfast for everyone, but no one woke, even with all our banging around the kitchen. I built up the fire and we ate alone, perfectly happy, then fell into bed, perfectly happy, and woke, perfectly happy. We stayed perfectly happy, too, for a while, and even rediscovered our happiness after we lost it. Then it got away from us again, and now we'd never get it back. I looked at the bruised and lacerated skin of her face. It seemed impossible that she wasn't waiting for me back at her apartment or somewhere else. Anywhere else.

"You know I found those pants," I finally whispered. "That doesn't necessarily mean anything, I know." I leaned my forehead against her casket. "I often leave my pants in women's apartments."

I lifted my head and touched her broken nose, her lips. They were unyielding. There seemed to be some frost on them, some freezer burn. I kept petting her and feeling how far away she was, feeling as alone as I'd ever felt.

I kissed her forehead and walked back to the room with gold wallpaper, where Diana stood and pulled me into another embrace. "I want to spend a minute with her," she said, "before we go to the luncheon."

I'd forgotten about the luncheon, forgotten that people would be there—friends, family, I didn't know who. Cynthia wouldn't be there, of course. She'd be here, surrounded by pictures of herself. I'd be at a luncheon, with everyone who'd lost her, with everyone but her.

8

BURKE

I didn't quit Denny's right away, even though our mother left me almost twenty grand. I took some time off when she died, a few days here, a few days there, and all I could think about was Nikki. I knew she was probably dead, but if she wasn't, she was sure to know what happened to Cash. I was spending so much time with her pictures, it seemed like I already half knew her anyway, and if she was still alive, I thought she might be worth getting to know a whole lot better. I wanted to devote myself full time to finding her, but Billy shook his head when I told him I needed a leave. "Can't get by without you now, Burke," he said. "Not with Marlene on maternity and Sully back in the can."

Billy was a good man, had hired me not three weeks out of Huntsville as a dishwasher, and then promoted me to line cook. I could feel the heat build in his office back behind the walk-in. I never would've laid a hand on him in anger. I swallowed hard and walked away. That's what ate at me the next couple days—how I was trapped by the man's goodness. Most ex cons don't get one decent shot, and here I was considering walking from mine. It started to eat at me how desperate I was to hold onto my shitty job, half convincing myself I was lucky to be working at that fucking Denny's while my brother's killers roamed free. And with

Connie gone, with Cash gone, with our mother gone, what did I have to be so good for?

I fell off the wagon, studying Nikki's pictures with a bottle out in the Goat, feeling her alive in the night, but knowing in the morning they killed her, too. I was tired of answering to Billy and my probation officer. No one had done a damn thing about my brother's murder. I drove to Austin again, but there was nothing left to discover. I didn't know where else to search, until I learned about the internet from a waitress at work. I tracked Nikki to a newspaper in New York, the guiding hand of fate delivering her to me just like that, delivering us to each other. I was so overcome with emotion, learning she was alive, I could hardly contain myself, like getting someone the best present you could imagine getting them and then having to wait to watch them open it.

She was all business when she picked up the phone, until I said my name, and then there was a heavy silence before I felt the air go out of her. "*Burke* Chandler?" she finally said, and it was like a damn breaking inside me at the sound of her voice, my blood rushing so hard and fast as I told her how I'd been looking for her and how happy I was she was alive, feeling it right there on the surface of my skin, in my throat.

"I was sure they killed you, too," I told her. "Just sure of it."

"No," she said. "I'm—no."

I listened to her breathing, so happy, and she said, "Burke?" and I said, "Yeah," and she said, "*Burke* Chandler?" and I said, "Cash's brother, Burke—I'm right here."

"Cash's brother," she said, shocked, just like I'd been shocked at discovering her alive, and so grateful.

"I was thinking they done something to you like they done to him," I told her. "I made up these awful stories in my mind about it—you and Cash and what they done to him. And what I thought they done to you. Making you turn on him."

"I was gone then," she said. "When he—when they."

41

"I thought maybe you'd know something," I said. "Who or why or whatnot."

"I was in Chicago then," she said. "My aunt's place in Oak Bluff."

"Oak Bluff, huh?" and she said, "I didn't know what happened back in Texas."

She sounded just like she looked, even though she wasn't southern and I thought she would be. But she sounded just like she looked. Beautiful. I told her I could sit on the phone and listen to the sweet sound of her voice all day long.

She didn't say anything for a long minute, but I could hear her breathing.

I wondered if she was about to cry, thinking about Cash, bringing up all her old feelings. She didn't really know me yet, so it wouldn't be me she'd cry over. Not yet. "You okay?" I asked her.

"Where are you?" she said.

"The house we grew up in," I said. "He must have told you about me," and she said, "Yes," and I said, "I just want to hear the sound of your voice. Like honey."

"I'm not—I don't know what to say."

"Tell me about you and him," I said. "All y'alls time together. I'm just so glad you're alive. I worked myself into a state nearly."

"This is just such a surprise," she said, her voice trembly and scratchy under all that honey.

"Did he bring you home to Waco?" I asked.

"Un-unh."

"So you never met our mom? She passed, by the way. Last month."

"I'm sorry," Nikki said. "I never did get to meet her."

"But he must've told you about me," I said. "We was close as could be. My time at Huntsville was done for him. Did he tell you that?"

"Yes," she said, and I said, "What'd he say, exactly?" and when

42

she didn't answer, I said, "You probably want to tell me face to face, is that it?"

That's when she finally let go, crying.

"It's all right," I told her. "I'm here now. You can let it all out."

That was probably the peak, when I was still too stupid to see what was right in front of me, right when I could feel us coming together, like I always knew we would.

"There's just so much we need to say to one another," I said when she was about done crying. "And I bet you're even prettier now than you was back then."

"Oh, I wouldn't. . . ," she said, sniffling, and I said, "I would," and waited for her to laugh, this long pause hanging heavy in the air between us.

Looking back, that's when something started feeling just a tiny bit off.

Nikki

When I finally got off the phone, I had to leave work and settle myself out on the boardwalk, walking, wanting to throw up every time I looked right at it, so not looking right at it, and nowhere to go, just walking, moving. Alina was probably home, packing for school, and Kyle was probably in his studio, preparing paintings for his upcoming show. I just wanted to go, to run. But where? I wasn't a kid like when I ran from Austin, from Providence, from Manchester. And I wasn't going to run from Kyle.

There was a guy I met when I was pregnant in Portland, Bobby, who I became close to before and after Alina was born, who loved me and loved Alina until she was almost two. He was thirty years older than me. That's when I realized how fucked up I was. Not the rape. It wasn't that. I wasn't even calling it that then. But just everything. My mother and how I'd run from her. Cash dead and Alina. My cousin Melanie in love with Daryl down in Austin, and how much I'd wanted him, how wrong that was, and how I wanted to be better than I was. Just all of it. And this guy, Bobby, in Portland, he loved me, I knew that. He loved Alina. And he was a good man—I liked him—but he wanted to be more than friends, which was perfectly natural, even though I didn't feel that way. And even though I didn't feel that way, I wanted to feel that way and made the mistake of trying. We slept together a couple times—twice—how I realized my feelings were never going to develop. I wanted them to, but there was nothing there. We lived together awhile as roommates, until I understood it was a kind of torture for him, that as long as I was around he'd hold out hope that we'd wind up together. I knew I was holding him back, that my presence in the house was hurting him. I'd never be able to give him what he deserved. I knew how much he wanted me to love him and I tried. But I couldn't do it, and he'd never find someone if I was around.

I was taking classes at Portland State and he'd take care of Alina while I was at school. I came home one night and he was in the kitchen just beaming, because Alina had called him Daddy, and even though I knew it was the best possible thing for Alina to stay there with him, because he'd love her and take care of her, and love me and take care of me, something snapped in me. I knew that minute I couldn't stay. I wasn't going to be taken care of. I didn't love him like that, and if I stayed one second longer I was never going to leave and we'd end up getting married and raising Alina and I would shrink a little every year and lose pieces of myself until there'd be nothing left. But wasn't that what happened to everyone? I was too young to know. I only knew I wasn't going to have that life. I ran to Seattle and didn't look back. I was twenty years old and too wild and stupid to know better.

But now I wasn't so young. I wasn't so fucked up. And I wasn't going to be so fucked up. I just had to satisfy whatever

Burke wanted and get rid of him. Mostly, I had to make sure he never found out about Alina.

Before he called again, I tried to prepare myself, to anticipate him.

"I just can't stop thinking about you," he said when I picked up the phone a few days later, and I realized I hadn't prepared anything at all.

"You don't know how hard it is to heal in prison," he said.

I'd noticed in his first call how often he mentioned prison.

"All I can think about is that night," he said, "how they could have hurt you and how you might know something you don't know you know. You learn just about all there is to learn doing time, including the fact that sometimes you know things you don't know you know. That's the guiding hand of fate, protecting you or steering you towards knowledge, the reason I keep wondering about that night and people that might have been around and such before he was killed."

I hadn't realized in the first call that he might be insane. I couldn't tell if that made my situation better or worse. Or if he even was crazy. I said, "But I was gone by then. Up in Chicago," and he said, "Why'd you go there?" and I said, "Just—the breakup and everything," and he said, "You had it pretty bad for him, didn't you?"

Since he'd discovered where I worked so easily, I knew he'd find where we lived, too, though I'd changed us to unlisted after his first call. But Texas wasn't so far. Not far enough. He'd show up at work, if nowhere else, and I couldn't imagine how I'd hide my feelings if I had to see his face.

"You seeing anybody now?" he said.

I thought of how Cash would have responded to Kyle, his insane jealousy. On the other hand, maybe the prospect of a man in my life would push Burke away. Though it wouldn't have Cash. It would have made him meaner.

"Cash always said you two was wild," Burke said. "Going

down to the river after work at Stubb's, the two of you drinkin' and skinnydippin' and gettin' high."

"That was a long time ago," I said.

"Not for me, though," he said. "Prison stops time. For me, it's like yesterday. And now I find myself thinking so much about you, Nikki, almost like we know everything about one another through him."

I felt myself sinking, and if I didn't come up soon I was going to have to inhale everything around me, suck it all into my lungs and spit it out once I reached the surface. I made myself breathe. I said, "It's been good talking to you, Burke. Good to remember those times."

"It's a kind of haunting," he said, "not knowing what happened."

"It's probably what the cops thought," I said. "How he was running with bad people."

"Is that what you told them?" he said, and I said, "I didn't tell them anything, I didn't talk to them," and he said, "They didn't track you down?"

"I told you, I was gone," I said. "And if I'd been there when they killed him, they would've killed me too."

"That's what I'm so grateful for," he said. "Like the guiding hand moved you away for a reason. For later, maybe. For us."

I swallowed hard and kept breathing.

"I just want to learn about the woman he loved," Burke said. "But not like this, a thousand miles apart."

I would never be able to look at his face.

"You don't need to be afraid, Nikki," he said. "I hope you know that much. I want to learn about your love is all, and everything about you. Ain't no reason to be afraid."

That's when I felt the old coldness—down deep. Just how he said I shouldn't be afraid. Like he could smell it on me. Like he'd been smelling it for years.

"You wouldn't begrudge me," he said. "Would you? Sharing memories together?"

"I just want to get on with my life," I said.

"Cash did, too," he said, "but they took him from us. And now it's up to us to honor his memory, the least we can do. Who knows what other chance we'll get to make things right."

"I just need some space," I said, and he said, "We gotta heal each other, Nikki," and I said, "I need time to think," and he said, "There's not one reason in this world we can't help each other, Nikki. We're practically family. Practically blood."

I should have gone to Kyle right then, the only one who could have helped me. I wanted to. I was going to. But I'd been taking care of myself all my life, me and my mother, me and Alina. And I didn't know how to tell it right. Besides, maybe Burke wouldn't call back. Alina was oblivious, packing for school, and I didn't want to burden Kyle with it. I didn't know how to tell it so he'd understand. I didn't know how to do anything but run, and I wasn't going to run. Not this time. Being off the phone made me think, each minute that went by, that Burke would just disappear and I'd never have to think about him or his brother again. I knew it was a lie, like I knew he knew everything that had happened between Cash and me and was just stringing me along, waiting for me to show my throat. But I kept telling myself the lie, like a song stuck in my head I hated and couldn't get rid of.

9

BURKE

I didn't want to believe she done it and didn't believe it, but the suspicion would creep up on me, the guiding hand turning my head to something I didn't want to look at, things she said or how she said them, like the fact that there wasn't no Oak Bluff, Illinois, at least not according to Rand McNally, though maybe I heard it wrong, because I knew she loved him and would love me, too, especially with him gone and me the person most like him in the world. But then it seemed like she just wanted to push me away—maybe because she was still so hurt, I couldn't tell. And I didn't know how to test it without pushing her further, which I didn't want to do. She was all I had and wanted in the world.

I told her that a few days later, that she was all I had and wanted in the world, and she said, "You don't know me," and I said, "I know you," and she said, "But you don't. And I can't keep talking like this. I've got work to do."

Knowing how much they loved one another, it didn't make sense that she wouldn't want to rekindle it. That she'd deny me. "I just want to share memories," I said. "Of Cash and the two of y'all together."

She held her tongue.

"It'll help the both of us," I said, and she said, "I want to get past all that."

I couldn't half believe she'd deny him now, everything they'd been through, everything I'd been through for them. Didn't she realize she never could have had him in the first place if it wasn't for me doing his time? I knew there'd been trouble between them, sure, but there was two sides to all that lovesick talk in his address book. And pictures don't lie, the way they'd moon over one another.

"You'd be surprised how alike we are," I said. "But, remember, I'm the older, so you'll come to realize, looking back, that it was always me you was seeing in him. You'll come to realize I was always the one—"

"I can't do this," she said. "I just can't do it," and she hung up the phone!

I called her back and she said it again, that she couldn't do it, and I said, "What about my hurt?" and she said she knew, she knew, but she couldn't help me now.

"How about I call back in a few days," I said, and she said, no, no, she didn't want to talk. She needed space. She was hurting too much.

"When then?" I said.

Nothing but her scratchy breathing.

"I got to see you," I said.

"No," she said.

I felt her slipping the same way Cash felt her slipping—how easy it was for her to disappear—and I said, "How come you never talked to the cops about what happened? How come they didn't track you down?"

"How would I know?" she said.

"How come you didn't go to *them* then?"

"I don't have to answer to you," she said. "Or anyone. I'm sure Cash told you that, too—that I don't answer to *any*one—so if you think for one goddamn minute. . . ."

I pulled the phone from my face, her awful sounds coming through the receiver into the air of my mother's kitchen. I think that's what sealed it more than anything, just the mouth on her—that queen bitch tone—like I was less than nothing, and she'd just been putting up with me in my time of pain and suffering. That goddamn filthy mouth on her.

I lowered my mother's phone to the cradle, holding everything tight, and stood from the table, pouring myself a cup of coffee with Jack on top. I walked my mother's house and tried to hold myself together.

The way she pretended not to know me, not to know Cash, fed this burning in me, hot and fast. But I didn't want to believe, even though I could feel how off she was in her voice. I didn't want to know, even though the guiding hand was trying to show me. So I fought it, the last time I fought it, because of what it proved to me over the next few hours and days, and then I never fought it again.

I knew the only way was to test her. And if she was true and it hurt her, we'd get over the hurt together and I'd make everything right. But if she wasn't true . . . I knew I'd feel so stupid for not knowing all along—what I learned at Huntsville—that it's almost always somebody close that'll kill you, my wasted worry nearly blinding me, the way she could turn on me after all my sorrow.

I poured another drink and dialed again. She answered and I sprung the test, because there was no other way to know for sure. "I know you killed Cash," I told her with gravel in my voice, praying it wasn't true as I placed the phone on the cradle, still trying to hold everything in.

I took a drink and then another, trying to calm myself. I still didn't know anything, even as I was starting to know in my heart, everything she took from him and me, everything clear and burning, shown by the hand. It was all too sloppy to be a Mexican drug gang. They would have made goddamn good and sure he was dead. The fact that she never went to the cops, never went to the funeral. All the lovesick talk in his address book. How she was probably using my sorrow against me. That was the worst of it.

I called again, praying I was wrong, but finishing what I started, already two steps ahead of myself, because if she was involved, I'd have to learn her level of fear—if she'd go to the cops, if she had a man who'd try to track me.

"I've been in prison fifteen years," I told her, "thinking about you. Cash told me who to look for."

She tried to interrupt and I told her to shut up. "I don't care for the cops," I told her, "but I'll go to them if I have to. I'll call them right now. I know you killed him."

I listened to her breathe, a sort of hiss, like air from a tire, and I waited, letting out rope in the silence.

"What is it you want exactly?" she finally said in this muted, broken voice.

I felt the beginning of my release, every muscle in my body settling, even as I felt the burning.

"Is it money?" she said, the guiding hand of fate fingering her once and for all and forever as the killer.

I was blind for a second before everything became red ringed and perfectly clear in the center.

"What is it you want?" she kept whispering. "What is it you want?"

"What do you got?" I asked her.

"Nothing," she said, crying and sniffling, but trying to stay quiet, trying to hide it.

"I guess you'd rather talk to the Austin police," I said. "Or the Rangers."

"No," she said, and then: "Ten thousand."

As if there'd never been a thing between us.

I hung up on her. Called back.

"Twenty thousand," she said. "Please."

I hung up and let her stew. Days passed as the hand worked out what would become of her.

"Let's start with an even fifty," I finally told her.

But money would never be enough. There'd have to be other payment too, worked out by the hand. I looked at her pictures in the Goat at night—waking up, it felt like, coming back to life after all my wasted years. I gave Billy one week notice and bought a plane ticket to John F. Kennedy airport, figuring I'd wing it until I spent some time with her. Now that I knew what she'd done to Cash, her betrayal and denial, I felt good doing right by him and our mother. It was like I could finally breathe on the outside free—a pure, true instrument of the hand.

10

ALINA

It's so unfair that it has to be Kyle when there are all these awful people whose deaths would make the world a better place, like serial killers and rapists, all the horrible people who hurt people, and I can hardly even believe any of it until I see her at the airport and fall apart completely, because it's so unfair that I'm never going to see him again, unless I believe in heaven, which I don't think I do believe, but maybe I do, though I don't think you can just decide to believe in something like that.

Mom doesn't look that horrible is what rubs me so wrong in the car on the Cross Island, like she's only comforting me and hasn't been crying for days. She tells me again what happened—a motorcycle accident on the Ocean Parkway, which I already know, and this rich woman, Cynthia, who my mother obviously hates, which is weird because she doesn't get jealous, and I'm like, "He was cheating on you?" not sure if I hope he was or hope he wasn't, and she's like, "I don't think so," but it's so obvious she's lying.

"Was it over between you, then?"

"Why do you say that?"

"Why was he with that woman?"

"I told you, they were friends."

"And you didn't like her."

"I didn't know her."

Everything she says is a lie. For the first time, I can recognize it, and that feels kind of cool, just that I can tell, but also horrible, and then I remember I'll never see Kyle again, and I wish it was me instead of him, or me with him, the two of us dead together, since my mom hardly even cares that he's dead. She was at school with me for two nights and then I was alone two nights, with Cassandra, my roommate, who seems really nice, but I was also missing home and my mom and Kyle, even knowing he was coming to Interlochen next week, our secret, unless he told her, which I know he didn't because I'd be able to tell, but now he's dead and I'll never see him again. She tells me about this lunch we have to go to with the families—right this second, so I'm not even going to drop my stuff off—and I'm like, Are you kidding me? But I see how hard she's trying to keep from crying, her face gone bloodless, and I feel it all coming up from wherever I'm holding it, and I can't hold it any longer, and she lets go, too, both of us crying all the way to Rockville Centre, where this stupid lunch is going to be, and that makes me feel worse, or just so guilty because of everything I felt for him but didn't mean to feel, just how he was coming to visit and how she never seemed to give him what he needed, but her crying now and feeling it with me, both of us crying now all the way to Rockville Centre and this stupid lunch.

MARK

I didn't expect to see Nikki at The Pavilion, seated next to Kyle's father, big fat Gino Pantopes. People weren't telling me the plans, or I was forgetting them. Nikki looked nearly as worn out as Cynthia had, her face drained and washed out from crying.

She didn't know anything yet.

The Pavilion was a wedding mill, with fountains and cherubs and a dining room upstairs offering a view of the rolling lawn and duck pond out back. Cynthia's sister, Beth, sat between me and her broker husband, Craig, who Cynthia had always called Dreg, and Nikki sat across the room with Gino and a girl who had to be her daughter. Plates of food appeared and disappeared. I thought of how Cynthia would have hated this event, how we'd have mocked it together, the duck pond and Gino's fat purple face and Dreg asking stupid questions. If I could have told her anything, I'd have told her how much I hated her and Kyle being remembered together like this. I didn't want to be that petty, but I was. I looked at Nikki across the room, entirely self-contained, and then I heard my name and noticed Denys standing and looking at me.

They were all looking at me.

"So, that's fine," Denys said. "Diana and I want to provide these opportunities to share our memories of Cynthia and Kyle. We thought you'd start, Mark."

I looked at my untouched plate, felt heat rush to my face. What could I possibly share about Cynthia and Kyle?

"I thought we'd go around the room," Denys said, "each of us—"

"Oh, God, no!" Celia Pantopes wailed.

She was half out of her seat, Gino trying to pull her down. When he lost his hold, she stumbled out the door, wailing.

I got away from my table before anyone could stop me.

Denys said, "Well, we don't," and Diana said, "Please, everyone, finish your lunch."

I followed Gino out the door, Celia struggling down the winding staircase.

I stood against the railing above them, watching them, unsure where to go.

Nikki came out of the banquet room, leading the girl she'd

been sitting with, her daughter. She stopped to introduce us, and I stuck out my hand like a car salesman. "Mark Barlow," I said to the girl, startled by how much she looked like her mother.

"We're going out back for a minute," Nikki said. "To get some air."

It seemed like an invitation. I followed them down the staircase, past Gino and Celia hunched by a fountain in the lobby. I stopped to take off my jacket, then caught up with Nikki and Alina on the manicured lawn.

"Because I want to is why," Alina said, snapping her hand away from Nikki and storming toward the duck pond.

Nikki seemed surprised to see me. "She's upset," she said, and I said, "Who wouldn't be?"

Nikki looked away. "I know," she said.

"I'll leave you alone," I said, and she said, "Stay."

We sat on a bench in the shade of an oak tree, watching Alina make her way around the pond. "She seems like a nice kid," I said.

"She is nice," Nikki said.

A fountain of water sprayed up from the center of the pond. Nikki massaged her forehead with her fingertips. "This whole thing's so weird," she said. "I don't know what to say up there. About Kyle. About the two of us."

"It's not like you're going to reveal some secret," I said.

She looked across the water at Alina half way around. "Secret?"

"You know," I said. "Everything you suspect or whatever."

She looked at me and sort of shook her head—like, *We're not doing this*—then looked away again. Fine by me. I didn't know anything anyway. Not for sure. Long seconds passed. I had a memory in my mouth of Cynthia's freezer burned forehead, even as I smelled Nikki through the humidity, vanilla or cinnamon, some kind of spice.

"This thing tomorrow," she said. She stood and scanned the

lawn, raising herself on tiptoes to look across the water, then sat back down. "I hope you don't mind if I don't go to Cynthia's service. It just seems crazy to me—doing them one after another like that at the funeral home. I know they were friends and everything."

"I'm not going to Kyle's either," I said.

We looked back to the pond, and then I couldn't help myself: "What do you think they were doing on that motorcycle, anyway—after midnight on the Ocean Parkway."

She shook her head.

"You don't wonder?"

She looked away.

"My mind keeps circling that," I said. "All the stuff we'll never know."

"There's plenty we'll never know," she said. "And they were close. So what?"

"I just want to know *some*thing," I said. "Where they were going. Where they were coming from. Anything"

"It doesn't make any difference," she said, and I said, "But still."

I heard a woman clear her throat behind us and turned to see Cynthia's sister.

"There you are," Beth said.

The women embraced, Beth looking at me over Nikki's shoulder as her eye makeup started to run. I knew Nikki had to know something. Just by how careful she was, how she pretended not to care. She had to wonder what was going on between them, even if she didn't care. And her knowing and not caring made my knowing and caring seem more stupid and pathetic, her strength or indifference—or maybe just privacy—somehow feeding my weakness.

NIKKI

Back in the banquet room, his eyes are on me all the time, something empty behind them, like part of him drained onto the lawn outside, and whenever I look up, whenever I wake from myself, there he is, looking at me. Cynthia's family surrounds him, and rich people come and go, as if he's been coronated, which makes me sort of sick, to think he's been elevated by her death, but I'm probably just projecting that because of how disconnected I feel from Kyle's family. Maybe her family's always been like this with him, having taken him into their wealthy embrace long ago, something always so horrible in me regarding rich people and their money, because, I'm sure, of how the lack of it has governed my own life. Even now. Especially now. I look to his eyes fixed on me over Diana's shoulder as she hugs him, and it's like he's lost, like he's calling for me.

Alina reaches out to me, and I squeeze her hand, both of us strangers in this room full of rich people, and shy, the only reason she clings to me. Burke said he'd arrive next week, and I still don't have a plan for the money, still don't know if I'm going to run. My job selling ads for the paper has led to writing reviews and interviews lately, the arts editor practically promising a move to the editorial side of the paper. I'll never find a job as good if I run again. I just need to get to Kyle's studio and see what I can find. It's possible he's got money stashed or something to sell, if the place hasn't already been emptied by Celia.

"When can we go?" Alina whispers.

"Soon," I tell her, petting her hair. She drops her head to my shoulder.

Cynthia's sister is pretty and flushed, and she keeps touching Mark, holding his hand, while the rich people say whatever they say to him and he looks at me. I wonder what he wants from me, what he has that the rich people want to touch. He obviously knows what I know, that there was something between Kyle and Cynthia, the way she touched Kyle the night the four of us ate together downtown, her hand on his arm, his shoulder, looking for a reaction from me every time she touched him. And her eyes in his paintings, too. I didn't care. I didn't have anything invested that could be taken away, part of why I should have just let him go, so they could have had each other. But I also wanted to love him like I hadn't loved Bobby in Portland. I've been too careful too long, holding myself too tight. Mark was going to let it eat him alive, the way he looked at their hands on the table that night at the restaurant, the way he questioned me just an hour ago on the lawn. I didn't care where they'd been or where they were going the night they died. Kyle and I loved each other—but I didn't own him and he didn't own me. We didn't owe each other anything, except kindness and respect. But that thought makes everything so much worse, rubbing it in my face again, how I held him back and kept him from the real love he could have had with Cynthia. I put my hand to my face, shading my eyes, and let myself feel it all in this room full of rich people, trying not to shake Alina's head on my shoulder and failing.

She runs her hand up and down my back, sniffling, "Can't we just go?" and I pull myself together and say, "In a minute," because I haven't spent enough time with Kyle's father. I don't want to close any doors.

I watch the rich people come and go, Mark looking at me like, Get me out of here, and for just a second, I see myself in that look, a sort of recognition washing over me, and I wonder if maybe, with all the rich people around him, if maybe—because it's only fifty thousand, impossible for me and nothing to them, Burke out there waiting to be paid, what I have to take care of before I can feel or do anything else, but as I look at Mark still looking at me, as helpless as I am, I dismiss the possibility of asking for anything, promising Alina and myself in my head, almost like a prayer, that we'll be okay, we'll be okay, we'll be okay, that we'll survive this bullshit with Burke unscathed, intact, that we'll come out of it stronger and better than ever. And then I'll let myself feel the loss of Kyle and forgive myself, maybe, hopefully. But Mark won't stop looking at me. And I can't tell if I recognize something in him or if I'm just seeing money.

11

BOBBY

Nikki was just a kid when we met, and I was approaching middle age, but she had a presence that made her seem much older, probably because of her mother being sick throughout her childhood. She showed me one of the crazy letters—her mother writing about flying to Portland in her ruined body ship—and told me a tiny bit about her childhood, but whenever I pressed for more, she'd shut me out completely.

It took a long time to get to know her and there was plenty I never did know, whatever it was she kept locked down so tight. She wouldn't tell me where she lived for months, and when I did find out, I couldn't believe she was staying in such an awful place. I asked her to move in with me, practically begged her, even though there was nothing romantic between us. And even though she said no, she let me walk her home that night, a first. She made us tea and sat me on her couch and put my hand on her belly to feel Alina kick. I told her I loved her. She looked at me a long time and said, "I know you do, Bobby." She was the only person who called me Bobby since kindergarten. She kissed me, another first. We kissed each other. "I love you, too," she said, but I knew her love for me was less than mine for her. It didn't matter. I would have done anything for her.

Later, when she was going to school at night, leaving me with Alina—who I loved as much as Nikki or myself—all I could do was give her space and try to hold on, which was impossible. I knew I was coming on too strong, my love becoming desperation, a repellent weakness, but I couldn't stop myself. You can't make somebody love you the way you want to be loved, and you can't stop loving somebody the way you already love them. You can try to hide your love, but it won't do any good. And I was never able to hide anything. Nikki hid everything. I heard her crying in the tub one night maybe a month after Alina was born, these coughing, choking sobs she was trying to contain, breaking my heart for her, but when I asked about it later that night, she pretended nothing was wrong.

"A lot of women get depressed after they have a baby," I told her, "because of their chemistry—a change in their hormones. My mother had that with my brother."

"I don't have that," Nikki said. "I don't feel that way."

"What do you feel?" I said, and she said, "Do we have to talk about my feelings?"

She smiled her radiant smile at me, her whole face lighting up. "Come sit with me on the couch awhile," she said. "Everything's good. Everything's fine."

We watched TV together, talking and laughing. There were times I could hardly stand to be in the same room with her, I loved her so much. But those feelings mostly came later, when I knew I couldn't hold onto her. Earlier, it wasn't so clear.

Before bed that night, she said, "Are you feeling better?"

"I was never feeling bad," I said. "You were."

"I wasn't feeling bad," she said.

Neither of us moved from the couch.

"Do you want to sleep in my room tonight?" I asked her. "Nothing has to happen. It would just be—you know—for the warmth. Or whatever you want."

"I don't think that would be smart," she said, and I said, "I think it would be smart," and she smiled again—you'd do anything to make her smile like that—and even though she didn't follow me into my room that night, she did follow me a month or so later, and I was able to delude myself for a while that she was falling in love with me.

Later, after she left, I kept a picture of the three of us on my bureau, taken when Alina was ten months old and we'd gone to Mount Hood for the day, Alina perched in one arm against my shoulder, and Nikki wrapped in the other, all of us smiling on the stone steps leading up to Timberline Lodge. I never tired of looking at that picture. I hoped Alina had a picture to remember me by, too, but even if her memories of me had faded to nothing, my love for her grew stronger—which helped me overcome my loss. I didn't blame Nikki for leaving like she did. She was the most private person I ever knew. And I kept trying to get her to open up, knowing I was pushing too hard, unable to stop myself. The least I could do was give her space to get back in touch with me if she should ever so want to, which she never did—my own fault and nobody else's.

I marked Alina's birthday each year with a trip to Timberline or Cannon Beach. Every girl in Pioneer Square reminded me of them, the girl Nikki had been and the girl Alina was becoming, the two of them sort of passing each other in my memory, crushing me and filling me all at once. Love like that's a blessing, whether you can hold it or not. And even though I couldn't hold it, I kept my love for them pure in my heart, careful not to spoil it with bitterness or regret, the sweetest joy of my life.

12

BURKE

I landed at Kennedy Airport a week before I was due, people in the rent a car line bitching about the heat and humidity, but it was nothing compared to Texas. Every minute since Nikki and I talked was a minute I spent wondering where she was and what she was up to, and what she thought I might do to her in the days ahead. I studied the map of the island, guessing it'd be like Corpus, with hotels everywhere, and since it was my first vacation in years, I figured I'd be staying in one of them swank places with a tiki bar on the sand. But there weren't hotels like that. A dude at a gas station directed me to the Royalty Motor Lodge on Sunrise Highway, with microwave ovens and refrigerators in the rooms, cable porn and patio decks, whores coming and going for the short stay rate and a liquor store less than a mile away, all of it just about perfect. I sat on my patio deck mixing vodka and Coke, looking at pictures of Nikki and feeling part of this movement sweeping me along, jangly and coiled, like when you've just crested the rise on a roller coaster and are about to go swooping down. There was a lot of light left in the day. I thought about trying to score some blow. I was all peaceful and wired and calm up there, perched on the edge of my future, as happy as I'd been in I don't know how long.

13

NIKKI

The boat's all the way out in Port Jefferson and belongs to a friend of the family, Burl or Merle or somebody, forty-some people on this enormous white boat motoring out to the Sound on a perfect, ninety degree day in September, what feels like the last day of summer. Alina can't stop crying, and I've been crying too, but time's running out and I hate myself for scheming about how to approach Gino, wondering if I should just take Alina out of school and run. If Burke finds out about her, I don't know what he might do, don't know if he'll try to claim her by proving me an unfit mother—a murderer. There's no reason for her to know any of that ugly past. I don't ever want her to wonder whether she came out of love or not. Because she did come out of love. Mine. I sit with her on a white cushioned seat at the back of the boat, way out in the Sound, as Celia tips the urn, what looks like a martini shaker, blubbering, Kyle's ashes floating into the air, up and swirling before settling over the boat's wake and dissolving.

MARK

I saw Nikki in the long hallway of the funeral home between services, carrying herself like Bianca Jagger, beautiful, distraught, strong for the moment, on the verge of collapse. I wondered how much she really knew, how much she cared. She'd been devastated the night we learned of the accident, but she seemed too self-contained to ever *need* anyone, the way I once needed Cynthia. Maybe if Kyle had died alone or never been born, Cynthia and I would have found a way to be happy. Maybe we would have gotten married and had babies and done the things people do. A week before she died, the idea would have been laughable, but now I couldn't quite tell. Because now I kept reaching for her, even though she seemed to be everywhere.

The last day I saw her alive we attended a party at her parents' place in Cove Neck, a fund raiser for the Metropolitan Opera, a thousand dollars a head, fifteen hundred per couple. Out on the lawn, eating cake under an enormous white tent, Cynthia said, "This isn't going to last forever, you know."

"What isn't?" I said. We'd been there three and a half hours. It seemed like it already had lasted forever.

"This freedom," she said, "to do what we want."

The operatic music had finally ended and now professional partiers surrounded us, beautiful event-specialists in polka dotted clown clothes, on stilts, in sparkling leotards, the theme of the event being Summer Circus Spectacular. They smiled and laughed and blew noisemakers and wrapped the donors in purple boas, pulling them to the dance floor for booty-shaking to the bad, disc-jockeyed music. A contortionist contorted herself on a raised platform in one corner of the tent. It seemed obscene, something the authorities should be made aware of, but when I looked around the tent, I realized the authorities were all there.

"What freedom?" I said. We'd entered a stage in our relationship where every conversation, every word, was a potential fuse for the pending explosion.

"To get out of here," she said. "To walk away. Someone had to set this up, you know, draft a guest list, mail out invitations, hire caterers." She took a sip from her water bottle. "Then she has to wait for these people to leave. This is what adults do. Years ago, it was children to worry about. This is the same thing—waiting for the children to go to sleep, waiting for the sliver of day that's yours to breathe in. And I don't want to talk about kids again. You know how I feel. I'm just saying, there's an inevitability to things. Kids included. Kids especially."

I saw Diana in her gold lame dress, working the tent, touching ladies' forearms, men's shoulders, as she sparkled through the small talk, her face tight and radiant. She made her way toward us, greeting us each with a hug and a kiss on the cheek. I noticed Kyle across the lawn at a glass-topped table with Denys and a neighbor woman, Marilyn, whose husband had been murdered on the Long Island Railroad in a shooting rampage several years earlier.

"When did Kyle get here?" Cynthia asked her mother.

"I don't know, dear. He looks wonderful."

For once he wasn't wearing leather pants.

"Come on," Cynthia said.

"Go ahead," I said.

Across the lawn, Kyle stood to offer Cynthia his chair, then grabbed another one for himself. They talked. They laughed. She touched his leg, his arm, his hand. Marilyn, the neighbor with the murdered husband, looked like she was about to cry.

Cynthia's youngest niece, Tamara, approached me with a juice box. "Can you open this, Uncle Mark?" I punctured the box and handed it to her. She took a drink, staring at me, then wiped her mouth and said, "Do you know where the wind comes from?"

Cynthia sat adoring Kyle at their table across the lawn.

"The motion of the earth?" I said to Tamara.

"No," she said.

"Clouds?"

"No," she said. She took a hit of juice, then pointed over my shoulder. "Look up." I turned and saw the maples rippling.

"See the trees moving and shaking like that?"

"Yes," I said, and she said, "They wake up and start shaking."

"That's cool," I said, and she said, "I know it is."

Later, Cynthia and I walked to the Sound while Kyle gave her nieces rides on his motorcycle. She took my hand and told me she wished I was coming to Lake George for her family reunion. "The girls love you," she said. "I think they make Beth a better person—less selfish. I've seen that change."

We walked in silence for a while, until she let go of my hand and said, "I'm just so tired of everything we do," and I thought, Okay. Let's get this over with, and she said, "Drinking and looking at art and finding new ways to stimulate ourselves . . . when all we really need is babies." She took my hand again. "I think I've figured out what everyone probably always knew—that babies are just these fantastic love generators."

She laughed, and that threw me off more than anything. How long had it been since I'd heard her laugh like that? Usually there was something biting behind our laughter, something cutting or mocking, but this didn't sound like that.

"It's like they create love where there wasn't any before," she said. "Like they're responsible for all the love in the world."

"Huh," I said, and she said, "I think that's why people have them today—I mean, with birth control and everything, now that it can be a choice, a decision, which might seem bizarre or unnatural, but maybe that's a good thing. To be so conscious of wanting them. In the past, they were just byproducts of sex. Now, you're making this choice to devote yourself, to surrender yourself to all that possibility, all that joy. . . ."

She squeezed my hand and looked at me, and it seemed like we were different people, like we could still walk together, laughing, like I was already mourning her. Part of me wanted to believe her. All of me wanted to believe her. I smiled back, but I didn't know how to consider something so cosmic and unknowable— where love comes from—a consideration that seemed far beyond me. For the first time in months, it seemed possible, or even likely, that we would find a way back to each other. I was afraid to talk, to ruin the moment.

We reached the Sound and Cynthia stopped abruptly, squinting down the shore.

Marilyn, the neighbor with the murdered husband, was walking on the rocks and gravel above the waterline, the tinsel on her purple muumuu reflecting the setting sun and making bright cuts of light against her body as she picked her steps away from us. I imagined an enormous bird swooping down and carrying her away.

I turned to Cynthia and another look passed between us.

I looked back to Marilyn, watching her careful progress until she nearly tripped.

Cynthia squeezed my hand and let it go as Marilyn righted herself.

Maybe she would have been a good mother. I never would have believed it until that day. But maybe she would have been.

Somewhere on the road behind us I heard the accelerating whine of Kyle's motorcycle as he kicked through the gears. Cynthia and I stood watching Marilyn make her way away from us. I felt such tenderness between us then, all this repair, but we had another horrible fight that night at her apartment, and the next day she was gone to Lake George and I never saw her again alive.

Now, only a few weeks later, she was still gone, sort of, and I was at her memorial service, unable to shake the feeling that she was everywhere. And nowhere. Meagan Finnegan sang, "I Will Always Love You," a song Cynthia detested, and I was introduced as the boyfriend and placed by the casket, expected to speak. I'd written some words down and held them shaking on a piece of paper.

"So," I said.

Several hundred people sat looking at me, waiting.

I had no idea what to tell them. The words I'd written were ridiculous, idiotic. I couldn't speak.

"Cynthia," I finally managed.

I felt her presence, as if she were still walking with me on that last day, or maybe hovering up near the ceiling.

"Cynthia," I said, working my jaw, grinding my teeth.

All these people in front of me crying and waiting. Strangers, most of them.

I stood up there until Denys led me back to my seat.

14

NIKKI

I take Alina to Tara's in Port Jeff Station, where we order lobster and sit on the same side of a small table so I can hold her. She seems a little stronger or more aligned with me after the shit with Celia on the boat this afternoon, after I played my money card and failed. I hadn't meant to bring it up or didn't know I would, until after Celia dumped the ashes and threw the empty urn into the Sound.

"Why'd you do that?" Gino said, and Celia said, "What difference does it make?"

She stormed down the stairs and inside the boat, everyone looking out over the water, embarrassed. Gino glanced back at me and followed her. Alina was still crying and had to throw up again. She leaned over the edge, but there was nothing left. I rubbed her back, whispering in her ear, as she stared down at the water rushing by.

Later, Gino sat beside me, his face purple gray. I felt such tenderness for him then. I couldn't imagine losing Alina. She was sort of hiccup crying as she looked down at the water, and I was holding her dress so she wouldn't even think about going overboard, not that she would, and Gino said, "If there's anything we can do, Nikki."

Gulls floated above and behind us, their greedy cries sounding far away over the motor and water sounds. A minute or so passed. I wouldn't let go of Alina.

"There might be something," I finally said, "that would help a lot. . . ."

I looked at him looking at me, so much concern in his face.

"Alina's school," I said, thinking I'd start there and see what I could get.

"What about it?" he said.

"Maybe you don't know," I said. "About Kyle helping us with money for that."

"We can help, too," he said. "Until you get on your feet," and I didn't quite understand that, because it wasn't as if we were going to recover from this experience and somehow end up with money as a result. I said, "She has scholarships and other help. I don't know what Kyle told you."

"Just what Alina told me," he said. "What you told me. Art school. Will ten thousand be enough?"

"Ten thousand?" Celia said, hovering behind Gino, her black, flapper dress sausaged over her.

Gino turned to her. "Don't, Celia."

Alina lifted herself from the edge behind me. I clenched the hem of her dress.

"I've never approved and you know it," Celia said, looking only at me, her makeup starting to crack. "I told Kyle he was a fool to give you anything."

When I was younger, I might have pushed her right off the boat and into the water. I really might have. So maybe I had gotten somewhere.

"Please don't do this," Gino said.

I knew it was Celia's money, that anything Gino could give would have to come through her. At least Alina's tuition was paid through the term. At least I could hide her that long.

"Kyle was generous to a fault," Celia said.

"Celia," Gino said. "Please."

"The free ride's over," she said, turning and walking into the boat, and Gino said, "Of course we can help. Will five thousand be enough?"

"Yes," I said. "Anything helps."

"What was that?" Alina asked as Gino walked away.

"Nothing," I said.

But she brings it up again at Tara's.

"Why does Kyle's mother hate you?"

"I don't know, baby."

"What did you do?"

I hand her a cracker she crumbles on the table.

"I don't think I did anything."

"Then why does she hate you?"

"Maybe she's just so sad. Or jealous maybe."

"Jealous?"

"Maybe."

"Of what?"

"I don't know. Kyle's love?"

"Because he loved you more than her?"

"I don't know," I say, because love is never equal and is not about measuring, and I never made any promise. But I did love him, in my way. I did.

"You don't know anything," Alina says.

"There's no reason to be nasty."

"Maybe there is," Alina says, and I say, "What reason is that?" and she says, "If you don't know—" and she starts crying again, but lets me hold her, lets me rub her back, her neck, her hair. She's just so spent from all the crying and puking, from everything she's been feeling.

The lobster arrives, Alina collapsed and sniffling against me. They serve it on paper plates and it's only five bucks because the drinks are so expensive. Alina can't eat it. Neither can I. We sit looking at it a few minutes.

MARK

After the service I rode with Denys and Diana and Beth and Craig in a Rolls limo to the cemetery, where I threw dirt on the coffin, sweating through my best suit. I rode with the same people to the Dayton's house, where there were hundreds of mourners, Cynthia's friends, some of our friends from college, but mostly business associates paying respects to Denys. I found myself on a couch, staring into the cleavage of Laurie Franks, a friend of Cynthia's from work. She told me what a great couple Cynthia and I made. She wrote down her number and put it in my shirt pocket, in case I should ever need to talk.

I got another drink, even though I was already drunk. I checked my phone and saw two missed calls from my ex-girlfriend, Liz. We'd worked together in Chicago. She'd been leaving messages lately about an old problem that had resurfaced. I had no intention of calling her back.

At the bar, the Dayton's neighbor, Marilyn, put her hand on my arm as I picked up my drink. "She was a good girl, Mark," she said. "You can take comfort in that."

"Yes," I said. "I do."

"Kyle, too," she said. "Very good people."

"Yes," I said, and she said, "I know a thing or two about loss."

I didn't want to hear about her husband again, but I looked at her face as she told me about Cynthia and Kyle and her murdered husband and everyone else in the world who was gone from us, unreachable. I didn't dare tell her Cynthia seemed more reachable than she'd been in a long time. Marilyn didn't want to hear that kind of talk. Nobody would want to hear that kind of talk.

"Good bye," I said to her after she ran out of things to say.

"Good bye," I said to Denys and Beth and Diana and Laurie Franks.

"Good bye," we all said to each other. "Good bye. Good bye."

ALINA

I'm not going back. I heard what his mom said on the boat and I'm not going back. So what if it's paid for, I'm not going back. She takes me to this bar after I've thrown up all day and we order lobster. As if I'm going to eat. And she won't tell me what really happened, why his mother really hates her, though maybe it is jealousy, which makes me so sick because of how much he loved her, and she doesn't even care, never cared enough, never really earned it. She holds me and pets me and I know she loves me. But why didn't she love him enough? He'd probably still be alive if she did. He probably never would have gone anywhere with that Cynthia if she'd just been there for him.

We sit at that place and then we go home.

We get in her bed together. At least she doesn't talk. At least she doesn't ask questions. At least she doesn't mention school. Because I'm not going back.

BURKE

From my patio deck in the humid night, I overheard some talk around the pool and ended up with a whore named Cinnamon, who set me up with an eight ball of coke, plus some oxycontins for my back. I hadn't been with a woman since Connie left, and Cinnamon was as good as any and better than most. She wasn't all in a rush like most whores are, or fake or bored or distracted.

After half the coke was gone, she looked through the polaroids on the bedside table and asked if Nikki was my girlfriend.

"Was," I said.

"She's pretty," Cinnamon said, and I said, "Was. She's dead now."

Cinnamon frowned, studying the pictures. "Look how young you were," she said, confusing Cash and me.

Later, she asked what Nikki died from.

I could hear birds outside my patio door, singing.

"A stabbing," I told her.

"Jesus," Cinnamon said, and I said, "Jesus got nothing to do with it," thinking of all the ways I'd make her pay, Cinnamon so sweet and careful as she studied me.

"Who killed her?" she said.

"Never got caught," I said.

I set her up with a bump of coke, then one for myself.

"Like that guy on the Island," Cinnamon said. "Joel something. He killed like twenty girls before they caught him."

I reached over and grabbed the photos from the night stand, the top one showing Cash in his stupid cowboy hat, so young and happy and alive.

"He chopped them up and all kinds of shit."

The last time I saw him down at Huntsville I tried to warn him away from prison, told him to go on and get his diploma, even if he didn't make the NFL. He laughed. I would have slapped his face if I could have, him so young and dumb and full of himself, just like everybody before they get caught. But it meant a lot that he visited. And then our mother writing not a year later that he was killed by a drug gang, that both her boys was lost to her now, as if I was never getting out. It wasn't that she played favorites—just that her boys didn't turn out how she hoped. Which was why I tried so hard when I got home.

"What could make someone that evil?" Cinnamon said.

Looking at Nikki so young and pretty, I had to remind myself how heartless she was. I flipped through the pictures I'd flipped through a thousand times before. It was all just good luck and bad luck, the guiding hand moving you one way or another, and now I'd be her bad luck and she'd be my good. In some ways, not directly, but somehow, looking back, it seemed like she killed our mother too, because once Cash was gone, she seemed to give up on life, even with me on the straight and narrow them long months at that fucking Denny's. She just seemed worn out after Cash died, beat, and there was nothing I could do to change it.

"She's got that bone structure," Cinnamon said, pointing at Nikki. "What my mother called breeding."

I looked at the top picture, one of the half-naked ones down by the river. I'm not religious, but such a happy girl killing my brother seemed like proof of the devil, which seemed like proof of God, since they were brothers or cousins, whatever they was.

Cinnamon put her head on my shoulder. "When'd she die?" she said.

"Long time ago," I said. "Fifteen years."

"And you're still carrying it?"

She propped herself up and put her hand on my face, looked into my eyes.

We were pretty fucking high.

"I don't think I'll ever get over her," I said.

I took her breast in my mouth.

"That's the most beautiful thing I ever heard," she said.

15

GAIL

We had our share of trouble, more than most, and Nikki blamed me for everything, just as her father had, Nikki blaming me for cancer and Michael blaming me for Nikki, though all his blaming stopped once he disappeared, three weeks before she was born. I thought if he just saw the miracle of her eyelids, her hands, he'd come home to us, but I fought that feeling, knowing she was the reason he'd left in the first place. When I told him I was pregnant, he accused me of tricking him, saying I must have stopped taking birth control, which wasn't true. "So let's take care of it," he said, but I wasn't giving up on her now that I had her. I'd never heard of anyone getting pregnant on the pill—"A miracle," I told him—but he didn't care. I knew she was destined for something, given the odds she'd beaten. And what she turned into—ungrateful, spoiled, selfish—I blame on my cancer and her inability to love, Michael's poisonous gift from Vietnam.

I never blamed her for him leaving. She was a good girl, obedient, smart, beautiful. I trace my happiest moments back to Michael when we were so young and in love, and to Nikki when she was a little girl, before my twin Patty and I both got so sick. That's when everything turned—during those horrible months of illness. And when I got better, I still couldn't pick myself up, and then Patty died of it and mine came back in the other breast. So, yes, those were awful times, I admit as much. But what kind of daughter abandons her mother? That's the real question. After everything I did for her, everything I gave, Nikki ran without a word of thanks or goodbye, leaving me alone in that shithole on Spruce Street, my looks gone and everything else gone, too. She sent one letter from Providence, Rhode Island, one letter from Austin, Texas, and then not one word more. What kind of daughter?

It was Patty's girl, Melanie, who wrote that Nikki was pregnant, maybe a year after she ran. I was sick again and full of pain medicine, high and dying, but the news of her pregnancy lightened me—spiritually, emotionally, physically—and even though I'd given up on miracles long since Nikki's birth, the lightness of my spirit took physical form. I began to levitate, first in inches over my bed, then up toward the ceiling, and gradually out over Manchester and across the state to Claremont—where I'd grown up—and then down the valley, looking, I finally realized, for Nikki's baby. Because the truth I saw gleaming down from heaven was that the baby was mine to save. I sent letters to Nikki, explaining the damage she was doing to the unborn child, offering my assistance, offering the baby a home and a mother, but every letter went unanswered, not even a thank you for the gift I sent, a pink and blue receiving blanket. This is when a girl would want her mother you'd think, but not Nikki. Never Nikki.

The final letter explaining my condition—that the cancer was back and everywhere—was returned undelivered, no forwarding address, Nikki's silence proof that she didn't care whether I lived or died, that I was long since dead to her, and that she didn't care about her baby either. It was as if I'd done something to deserve such mistreatment, when all I'd done was hold my ground to bring Nikki into this world. She wouldn't even show me the baby before I died, wouldn't even acknowledge me. I wrote her that they were my genes in that baby too, that if it wasn't for me and the stand I took, the baby wouldn't exist at all, let alone Nikki, who I'd given up everything for. All I wanted was a picture of the baby, a lock of hair, anything. What I got was exactly nothing.

But in my dreams the miracles unfolded. I'd levitate over my old house near the Connecticut river and then farther and farther out, sometimes gone from my dying body for days, levitating across plains and mountains to Portland, Oregon, Michael joining me sometimes now, no sign on him of the agent orange poison that killed him, but both of us like we were in 1970, so young and fearless and in love, floating out over the country to save our baby.

NIKKI

Alina vomited all night, reminding me of my bus trip to Austin after I'd stolen money from a sweet drug dealer in Providence and felt like I finally had a chance in this world. I got sick on that bus, my eighteenth birthday, and threw up over and over, but I'd never felt so free—my mother and Providence gone behind, and no idea of Cash or Alina up ahead, Cash's baby, too, though his contribution was merely sperm and he was dead before I knew she was stitching herself together inside me.

It never occurred to me to try to save him. I didn't even know he was dying that night, and he did nothing to save himself. I drank for hours at the Top Hat, watching Daryl and his band and my cousin Melanie up front adoring him. I felt so sick for having slept with Daryl, knowing Melanie loved him, and sicker still for not being over him. He had a wandering eye, Melanie told me, and wouldn't commit to anyone, though everyone wanted him anyway, something I knew all about. I tried to drink my guilt away, but my gaze kept falling on Melanie adoring Daryl. She was the one I was close to, not him. She was the one who moved with me from Duval Street after Cash wouldn't leave me alone. I'd lock my door at night and he'd climb through my window, into my bed, until Melanie and I moved and he didn't know where to find me.

And then he was gone—I thought for good—and it was like I could breathe again after all those months of disintegration. Cash had been so happy when we met, a few days after I stepped off that bus in Austin, but as time passed and we got closer, he wanted more and more of me, pushing me away with his interrogation. Where had I been? Where was I going? "You don't know what love is," he kept telling me, and I started saying, "Find someone who does." I watched what he called his love for me turn him mean and ugly and small. That's what really killed him, all that hatred, all his clutching meanness. I remember crying on Melanie's bed, wondering what had become of us, when we'd both been so happy when we met, but he just kept coming, breaking into my room, until I felt nothing but revulsion. I slept with a baseball bat, and he kept coming. I threatened to call the cops, and he kept coming. Then Melanie got us a place and we moved when he was gone to Waco, and I found myself settling into a peaceful existence, which I ruined by getting tangled up with Daryl and betraying Melanie.

I stood watching her sway by the stage, so pretty and in love, but Daryl wouldn't look at her. He'd told her he didn't want a girlfriend. I knew what he wanted. Everyone knew what he wanted. And everyone gave it to him, something so magnetic in his voice or smile. I didn't want to be the person I was becoming, didn't want to love Daryl, who didn't deserve my love. I should have just been grateful to be safe with Melanie. I hadn't thought of Cash in days, so stupid to believe I'd shaken myself free, as though he'd let me walk away.

I saw him come into the Top Hat as Daryl was screaming the first line to "Blood Poisoning," my favorite song he sang, Cash crossing Daryl through the lights and smoke and filling me with so much anger and revulsion—because I hadn't seen him in weeks and thought maybe he was gone for good, back in Waco or in jail, even after all his threats. It was just so awful to see him when I was watching Daryl, thinking about Daryl, still wanting Daryl, even though I had no right to Daryl. I pounded my beer and ran, drunk and lovesick. I thought I was at least careful enough not to be followed. I went straight to bed, and when I woke, still drunk, he was inside me, and I wasn't aware anymore of hating myself, because I was just moving and moving, trying to get away. He punched me hard at the corner of my eye, over my cheek bone, the sting and then the throbbing in my face settling me into this quiet rage, this animal I was becoming as I reached for my jeans, pretending I was into the sex. I moved with him, pulling the knife from my pocket. I opened it and lifted it and brought it down and then it was just sound—all that rage in my throat—and white light as he ran, hobbling away.

Hours later—after I went looking for Daryl, and came home again, where I just wanted to be dead—I tracked Cash to the house on Duval, empty bottles of Percocet and Jack on the floor beside him. I knew he was hurt, but I thought it was the whiskey and downers that accounted for his lethargy. I chopped his finger at the top knuckle, the way I'd learned to cut chicken at Stubb's. I bandaged him, figuring we were even, and when Melanie called a few hours later to tell me he was dead, I was like, *But I let him live*, so arrogant and stupid, Alina's cells already working to bring her to life inside me. My only emotion was fear I'd go to prison, when I should have just gone to the cops. But I wasn't calling it rape even to myself then, and I knew the cops wouldn't call it rape either. Besides, I'd gone there to kill him and had killed him. I hated him more for dying than for the rape even, and once I learned I was pregnant, I hated him for that, praying all those months in Portland she was Daryl's.

But once I had her, it didn't matter where she came from, and it still doesn't matter and never will. Her flight back to Michigan was at nine this morning, though she didn't know that, and there's no way I can put her on a plane so sick and wrung out. She sleeps and sleeps, and I wander the house—stalled, waiting, weakening—the clock ticking down as Alina sleeps. If Cash hadn't come to me like he did, I wouldn't have her, I know that much, but that doesn't mean I go looking for pain and hurt and injustice to see where love might bloom. It doesn't mean I have forgiveness for him, either. It just means you can't know where love might come from or how it might rise in you, and how strange it is that it can bloom from a bed of hatred and meanness and fear, nearly erasing the bad that bred it. But it was easier for me, with him dead and gone from the world. If he were still alive, breathing my air and feeding my fear and weakness . . . which is why Burke has no right to anything.

MARK

I hadn't been doing well, hadn't been sleeping. Or maybe I'd only been sleeping. I drove to Cynthia's building, which had been a spice warehouse for a hundred years before its conversion to illegal lofts. The air was infused with these lingering smells, cloves and cinnamon and spices you couldn't name. Cynthia's answering machine flashed "12," eight new messages since I'd last been there. I wandered her place, opening drawers and handling knick-knacks, smelling everything. When I found a bottle of prenatal vitamins on her kitchen counter, I couldn't recognize what I was holding at first, couldn't understand the implications, even as evidence bloomed around me, pregnancy books and baby catalogs and a car seat by the door. Had her breasts seemed bigger the last time I'd seen her, before her trip to Lake George? I looked at the vitamins with her name on the bottle. Would she have told me if the baby were mine? Would she have known? Maybe there was a way she could tell, or just a wish, the final glue for her and Kyle.

I opened the window in the living room that led to the fire escape and gathered the baby books, the car seat, the prenatal vitamins. I crawled outside and dumped everything, piece by piece, to the alley below. I stood on the grated platform, looking down at the mess I'd made, feeling myself coming undone, like she'd come undone at the end of our last year in Providence. She'd had an abortion that fall, which made us sweet for a while, but we returned to our old routine soon enough, cheating and breaking up and getting back together. Maybe three weeks after our last breakup, I was at a party with another woman, Maya, and Cynthia walked in and saw us together. A shadow fell over her as she stood winding up. Maya must have seen the craziness in her eyes. "Go," I said to her, "I'll catch up with you later," and she headed for the back door as Cynthia came at me, scratching, punching, kicking, grabbing my hair in fistfuls. I picked her up and squeezed the breath out of her, and when she finally let go of my hair, I dropped her to the floor. The whole thing was over in thirty seconds, but the party had stopped around us, people looking on, horrified. Who could blame them? This kind of thing didn't happen to people like us. Would we kill each other?

I left the party and walked to Fox Point where I sat for hours, and when I finally got home, I heard Cynthia in my bedroom, crying. I opened the door and she was on the floor, surrounded by—I couldn't tell what. Rags, it looked like. I saw scissors beside her. She must have seen me see then, because she looked at them and shook her head. I realized she was surrounded by clothes she'd cut up and paper from books she'd torn apart and pieces of records and tapes she'd smashed, nearly everything in my room destroyed. But all the rage was gone. She looked wasted, drawn out, full of—I didn't know what. Grief, I guess.

"I'm sorry," she said, as I took in the damage, "I really am."

I saw how worn out she was.

"I know this is wrong," she said. She shook her head in the mess she'd made, staring at the floor.

I went and sat with her, knowing it was over between us for good. We both knew. She said she was sorry again and I said I was, too, and we sat together in the mess of my room for a long time. She started to clean up, but I told her I'd take care of it later. That was the weird part—how tender we were once we realized there was nothing left between us. But she got help and worked to make herself better and didn't blame me for her cracked ribs—though I blamed myself—and she got better. And we were apart all those years and probably should have just left it alone and never gotten back together in the first place, but she kept getting better and we did get back together and it was good for a while—until Kyle showed up and we started our old cycle.

I stood on her fire escape in the heat, looking down at the baby stuff I'd dropped to the alley, feeling myself slipping, the way she'd slipped that night in Providence so many years ago—but she'd come back. She'd gotten better. Her insanity was only temporary. And I'd played my role, like she was playing her role now, wherever she was. I went back inside, her cool, dark apartment sort of foggy or misty, and so quiet and still, except for the answering machine flashing on the kitchen counter. I walked to it and hit play, activating the voices from the past trapped there, a message from Beth, a message from her mother, a message from Planned Parenthood, twisting my guts, but all Planned Parenthood wanted was money. There was no planning, no pending parenthood, no mention of a recent pregnancy test or abortion.

I had this crazy feeling that the baby's voice was going to be on the answering machine with some kind of message for me. Or that I'd be able to track it down somehow on the internet, so I could determine its lineage—if it even existed, which, if it did, it really didn't, since it would have died with Cynthia.

The fourth message was at 5:50 on the night of her death, and I couldn't quite recognize his voice at first or make sense of it. He was supposed to be dead. And everything was so foggy.

"Hey, baby," he said. "It's me."

It took me a second, but then I knew.

I punched the stop button on the machine.

Baby?

When I'd found his pants in Cynthia's clothes, I was nearly sure, but not quite certain, and his voice was already on the machine, less than twenty-four hours old, waiting for me. But I hadn't listened.

I turned on the machine—"Hey, baby," he said—and turned it off.

They both seemed so far from dead, animated completely by my rising hatred and embarrassment and shame.

"Hey, baby," I said.

I started the machine.

Kyle said, "Hey, baby—"

Stopped it.

"What the fuck, Cynthia?"

Started it again.

"Hey, baby," Kyle said, "it's me. I was thinking about what you said, and I think I know a better place."

I had to stop myself from stopping it.

"Anyway, if you're free tonight, and you feel like it, we'll go for a ride and I'll show you. Nobody's ever down there, so it's like... Oh, and we'll bring binoculars. And I'll bring a blanket this time, to keep the sand out of our asses."

I was walking circles in her living room, listening to his voice. I lifted a potted plant by its wrist-fat stem and swung it until the plastic pot flew off, then slammed the root ball against a wall, knocking a shitty framed photo of Billie Holiday to the floor. I kept banging until there was dirt all over the place.

86

Another message came on the machine and for a minute I couldn't tell if it was me or the caller breathing so hard, and then I knew it was him again—his ragged, raspy breathing—maybe dead now, somehow calling from deathland. But as I made my way to the kitchen, I heard myself saying her name on the machine, my electronic voice so muted and small, as if a pallet of bricks was sitting on my chest.

I could hardly recognize this behavior as my own, so horribly intimate, so weak and tiny, after the fuck-lord's message. But it was me—calling Cynthia's machine when she was less than twenty-four hours dead—breathing and rasping and saying her name on the night I'd called to study her voice.

"Cynthia," I said on the machine, and again: "Cynthia." I kept calling. And breathing, as if I'd just run fifteen miles, chased by killers.

Or maybe it was me from the future, somehow calling from deathland.

It was my living breathing though, and my damaged voice, but all I managed in the last message was, "I," through all that breathing, and again, "I," and one more try: "I," before the machine clicked off.

16

BURKE

I nearly have a heart attack when I see her Monday afternoon, sitting on her stoop on Wyoming Avenue. I look enough like Cash that it's possible she'd recognize me, even if I am twenty years older than him when he died, but I never could have dreamed she'd look exactly the same as in the photos, though women have all kinds of surgeries today, and I only get a quick look before I push the rental car past. I park up the block and walk down the opposite sidewalk, wondering if it could possibly be her, so young and beautiful and horrible. The oxycontin I took for my back's made my head fuzzy, but walking south on the opposite sidewalk, I clock her again, positive it's her, reading a big book in the sun like she don't have a care in the world—like I'm not out in the world looking for her. Like I'm harmless. I pull my Mets cap lower, the bill practically resting on my sunglasses. Even though it's a hundred degrees, long white sleeves hide my tats. I shaved this morning, too, and now I'm not worth a glance from her, Miss high and mighty, Miss bitch heartbreaker. I can't remember a time I've felt so alive, my heart in my ears.

I walk down Wyoming to Ocean View, then up Wisconsin to Park and back down Wyoming. I left my mother's .38 at the Royalty, but I must outweigh her by a hundred pounds. It would be nothing to kill her with my hands. This is the smartest part of my plan—to make her think she won't see me till Friday, giving me all this time to figure out my surprise, directed by the guiding hand of fate.

She's still there on my next loop, even looks up from her book and sees me across the street. I wave. She waves back. She has no idea who I am. But I know exactly who she is. And the feeling is like when you're with a woman and know something good's gonna happen, maybe not right away, maybe not in five minutes, but soon, because she's already made the decision in your favor. And all you're doing is riding it home, Cash's killer laid out like a birthday present waiting to be opened.

ALINA

The western sun hits our little porch where I sit with *The Odyssey*—my stupid book for Freshman English—pretending to read, pretending I'll go back. I've been home three nights and haven't called Jen or Ashley, haven't even walked the beach. I overheard my mother this morning, rescheduling my flight when she thought I was asleep, after throwing up so much on that stupid boat yesterday. Wednesday's the day Kyle would've come to Interlochen, but she doesn't know that, because that's between Kyle and me.

Some creepy guy in a Mets cap waves from across the street. I wave back, feeling Kyle all around, protecting me.

He had a cabin booked through the Stone Center right on campus, and planned on staying at least two nights and maybe longer. It was why I finally agreed to go to Interlochen, his secret promise to visit, but now I feel tricked because I'm still looking forward to it, even knowing he won't be there and I won't be there, but my mind stuck on that cottage, maybe the two of us drinking wine and kissing in front of the fire, all the other girls so stunned to see me with an almost famous painter, so handsome and funny and never talking down to me. There's no reason whatsoever to go back now. I know I was just a kid to him, his girlfriend's daughter, but my mind keeps landing in that cottage and the wine and kissing on the floor in front of the fireplace, which might seem kind of creepy or sick, given our age difference and the fact that him and my mom were together and everything, but it's really just a thought my mind doesn't mean to have. Just a place I find myself returning to.

"What are you doing out here?" my mother says, startling me.

I crane my neck to look at her standing behind the screen door.

"Come in, baby," she says. "You'll burn."

"I'm not going back," I say.

"Alina," she says, stepping through the door. "I know how you feel."

"You don't know how I feel," I say. "And I don't care."

"Alina," she says, standing over me, and I say, "No," and she says, "Kyle would care," and I say, "Don't even say that."

"It's true," she says.

As if I don't know that.

"I want to tell you something," she says.

She touches the back of my neck, under my hair, but I can't look at her.

"I didn't want you to go at first," she says. "I know that sounds selfish, and it was selfish, I guess. But I wanted a few more years with you here at home. With me."

I count the cars in front of our house and up and down the street. I count the clouds and vapor trails above us. I didn't want to go at first, either. It was never really what I wanted, except that Kyle wanted it for me, and then it was fine by me, except I didn't want to be away from home.

"Kyle convinced me," she says, "of how important it was to cultivate your talent, to put it in a place where it could grow and develop—"

"Just don't," I say, and she says, "Listen, Alina. I'm trying to give you the chance we talked about. What Kyle talked about."

"Don't say his name," I tell her. "Don't ever say his name again."

"Get in the house," she says.

She snaps her fingers, points at the door.

I've never seen her like this.

"Right now!" she says, pointing and snapping and shaking.

I stand and carry my book inside, her pathetic little slave.

"Don't even think about slamming that door."

I close my door silently, hating her, deaf to her, completely and forever separate from her, then open it and slam it as hard as I can.

NIKKI

The hatred in Alina's eyes sends a panic through me, the same hatred I felt for my mother, and even if my mother was so manipulative and cruel, I regret now that I couldn't have been a bigger person when I was nineteen. I could have at least let her seen Alina before she died alone up in Manchester, or even gone and taken care of her. But I'd been taking care of her since I was nine years old, watching her hatred for everything living grow with her dying, and I wasn't strong enough to forgive her then. The thought of Alina carrying such hatred makes me frantic. I should just load her in the car and bolt, tell her something about my mother, how I realized too late how sick she was, how she wasn't always horrible, didn't mean to be horrible, though I couldn't understand that as a girl, couldn't recognize any good in her for so long because it was all killed by her sickness. Like Alina, I never met my father, but was frequently told what a great man he was, something I believed when I was very young and later knew had to be a lie. And then I hardly thought of him again. For so long I wanted nothing more than to get away from where I came from, but I never wanted that for Alina, always dreaded it—that she'd run from me the way I'd run from my mother. She slams her door and stays in her room and I wander the house, feeling my mother everywhere, her sickness and my smallness filling the air.

17

MARK

I walked to the bodega for cigarettes and beer and chips and dip, then stopped at the liquor store for vodka and whiskey. It was over a hundred degrees out, all this weather I had to wade through. I couldn't stop hearing my voice on her machine, echoing in my skull, "I . . . I . . . I . . . Cynthia." Back in her building, I couldn't breathe after the glare and stink and noise outside. I had to walk upstairs and unpack these bags in her kitchen. I had to hold on by pretending not to hold on, my skin itchy over its entire surface.

"Make a sandwich or something," Cynthia would have said. "Jesus."

The sandwich was a good idea. I ran up the stairs to her apartment.

"Don't be so uptight," she would have said.

I had to stop my aimless movement and concentrate on what was in front of me.

"Anyway," she would have said. "The weather's fantastic."

I ignored her.

"Really beautiful."

"Where's that?" I said, and she said, "Paris," and I said, "Really?"

"Maybe," she said. "What do you care?"

I concentrated on the sandwich, on bread and cheese and mustard and one tomato that wasn't rotten, chewing and swallowing, feeding, keeping everything away from Cynthia's prying eyes and ears. Keeping everything shut down tight. After lunch, I mopped the kitchen, then took a bottle of vodka up on the roof and started drinking.

It was cooler up there than on the street, and you could see Queens and Manhattan, the concrete and glass and steel rising toy-like off the island, tinker toys or sticks or blocks poking at the sky "in the gloaming," as Cynthia used to say, the sun making its way down the backs of the towers, Jersey on the other side of the rivers and Queens up there and the rest of Long Island behind us choked with traffic and exhaust and sprawl, the night falling and the city lights sparkling through the heat and humidity, the blinking red and white lights of planes rising and falling, planes over the city like insects waiting to land on the gigantic earth elephant. I wanted to call Nikki, but thought better of it. She knew nothing of what I knew now. I'd known for a while that Cynthia wanted children—it was woven into every word she'd said the last few months—but I never would have guessed she'd start having them without me, or that she'd get pregnant without telling me. If she had told me, she knew and I knew I never would have supported it—not the way we were before she died, disintegrating. Maybe now, drunk on her roof and hating her for going to Kyle when I wouldn't breed with her, when I wouldn't procreate or reproduce or whatever the fucking fuck—now, sure, now I'd go along with it, now that I could travel back in time and know that she'd breed with Kyle. But even as drunk as I was, I knew maybe the baby was mine. It was mine or it was Kyle's, but even if it were alive, it would really only belong to Cynthia and itself, such stupid thinking. I kept drinking, watching the lights of the city, filling myself, emptying myself, somehow managing to get back downstairs to Cynthia's bed without killing myself.

NIKKI

I sit up after Alina goes to bed, listening to last year's P.J. Harvey album, playing that song "Horses in My Dreams" over and over, almost crying with the repeated line she sings, "I have pulled myself clear," because I have pulled myself clear so many times and just have to do it this one more time. But I don't know how. I'm over-thinking it instead of just acting, responding, reacting like I always do, and so worn out from what I told Alina.

I asked her to help me cook and she stood in the kitchen pouting, peeling garlic, cutting an onion, an eggplant, but I didn't try to draw her out and we didn't talk, until I told her I understood her feelings and that she didn't have to go back to Interlochen. I opened a bottle of wine and poured her a glass, and at dinner I told her about my mother, her grandmother, how some animosity between an adolescent girl and her mother is normal, helps the child separate, but that what I'd felt was deeper, and I regretted a lot of those feelings now all these years after she died. And then Alina wanted to know what my mother had done that made me run

I sat for a long minute trying to find an answer, or the first words that would lead to an answer. But I couldn't find any words. The animosity felt impenetrable, even though it's softened over the years, maybe more lately, and I had to push at it for what felt like a long time to find a way through it.

"She was so sick," I finally told her. "That's what's always been wrong about my feelings. She was so sick, and I just left her—like she could have helped it. Like she wanted to be that way. I was nine years old and scared to death."

I told Alina how her hair had fallen out, how Aunt Patty was there to help at first, but my mother made her go away because she only wanted me with her through those long months of chemo sickness, and I wanted to be near her, but she would have me do all these chores, shopping, cooking, cleaning her body, and it was always wrong, the food inedible, the room never clean enough, making her sicker, she said. She let me know her reaction to the treatment, her wasting, was my fault, but she didn't blame me. She understood I was trying. She just needed me close to her in bed, where she'd hold me and baby me. She helped me knit a sweater for a doll part of me felt too old for already. Another part of me wanted that doll. She'd tell me she knew I didn't mean to hurt her, that it was her fault for breastfeeding me in the first place. She told me her breast had been filled with poison, and that the poison had gone into me as a baby, my bones and body already filled with it, and probably breaking down because of it, which scared me to death, as did the wound itself, the scar where her breast had been, which she wanted me to study.

"Do you see how sick she was?" I asked Alina. "How crazy?

Then there was radiation, after the chemo, and she wasn't throwing up anymore, but still wanted me near her all the time. She was drinking again, on the verge of losing her job at Velcro, and she'd hold me in bed, telling me I was the only thing keeping her alive, and as she held me, I could almost feel—I don't know— it felt like she was absorbing me, taking all of me from the inside out.

She lost her job and I started spending nights in my own bed, which was a relief, but also lonely—this is how pathological the situation was—until the cancer came back in her other breast, this when I'm twelve and trying to make my way in school, starting to think about boys, and it's right back to her wanting me in her bed, cleaning up after her because she was so sick from the treatment and drinking on top of it and throwing up the liquor. She'd hold on to me or make me take off my top so she could examine my breasts, and she'd say, "See what they'll do, Nikki? Look at me. Do you see?" Or, she'd say, "You're such a good girl, Nikki, the only one who cares." She'd wrap me in her arms and I'd have this horrible thought that she was trying to absorb me, take the life from me—but she was my mother, and I loved her, even as I pulled away, which I knew was wrong, pulling away, but I was so stuck—I wasn't strong enough—and what else could I do?

"It's okay, Alina," I said, because she was crying, because I'd scared her with the story, so lost in telling it, doing what I'd always promised myself never to do, to scare her with these awful stories. She came into my arms, crying.

"I don't ever want you to feel like you owe me anything," I told her. "That story's so old anyway. So far away and buried. I'm sorry I told you that."

My whole body was vibrating with it.

"But I want to know," she said, and I said, "I'll tell you more another time," and she said, "When?" and I said, "Tomorrow or another time."

I held her for a long time as she sniffled against me.

"Can I sleep in your bed?" she said, and I said, "You don't think that'll feel funny after the story I just told?"

She shook her head against me and I finally got her settled into bed and listened to P.J. Harvey singing that she's pulled herself clear. I still don't have any idea what I'm going to do with her. I need to get her somewhere safe while I deal with Burke. I wonder again if Mark can help, just the look I saw on his face at lunch, when he was surrounded by the money people and wanted nothing to do with them. He looked as lost as I feel now, all those people kissing his ring, and also—he just seemed, even with the rich people swarming him, entirely alone, which, except for Alina, is exactly how I feel.

ALINA

I feel so guilty I can't sleep, twisting in her bed, and she's snoring

97

and twitching and kicking, probably because she drank wine. I've known bits and pieces of her life, I've asked her to talk about it many times, and I knew there was some bad stuff, but I never realized how alone she must have felt, and that makes me think I've always only taken her for granted, and what if something happened to her? I just feel so guilty about Kyle. It didn't mean anything. But I did like him. I did love him. I do love him. And the other stuff was just thinking, just images and feelings that came to me. I probably should have told her he was coming to Interlochen, which feels like a dirty secret now, this thing I've been holding onto, but there isn't any reason to tell her now, because it might just make her mad or hurt, or it might make her think there's something really wrong with me, and I don't want to worry her like that. She hasn't even said anything about school, just that I don't have to go back to Michigan. Does that mean Long Beach High School? It's so late and I can't sleep and she won't stop moving and it was just a dream really, that's all—especially now—just a dream.

BURKE

I try to find my way back to that place in my mind where I kept the Goat and all that past, but I can't get to it, because it's used up and rotted, and I ain't supposed to need that anymore anyway, being on the outside free, but I can't sleep or rest at all. I felt so good seeing her on her porch I could hardly contain myself, but then Cinnamon wasn't around and wouldn't answer my calls, even though I scored another eight ball and sat on my patio deck as the day wore itself out, drinking vodka and doing lines off my hotel desk, the traffic like a river on Sunrise Highway and getting Cinnamon's goddamn machine every time I called from the payphone down by the ice machine. Back at Huntsville, Carl talked about the whore of Babylon getting stoned to death for washing Jesus's feet, but I can't remember if it was Him that saved her or Him that ordered her killed for touching His feet, or if maybe touching His feet was a good thing. I thumb through them goddamn pictures and wonder how I could have been so happy to see her, when now it feels like it took something out of me, everything, her on her porch so young and unchanged, as if life never touched her. Whores come and go by the pool while I drink, but none of them's Cinnamon or Nikki. I keep trying to make my patio deck the place I escape to, but I can't remember what Carl said about the place you escape to being the place you're already at, because the Goat's rotted behind me, Nikki so young and sweet like Cinnamon on her porch down in Long Beach, not in the Goat with me in the past, but on her porch in the Goat on my patio deck. I pray to the hand and Cash, Nikki all sweet and young and unchanged, Nikki and Cinnamon and Carl down in Huntsville, and me in the Goat on Cinnamon's porch—Nikki and Cash and my mother and me, and Nikki just the kid she was when her and Cash was me and Cinnamon, and I'm praying to the hand, like Jesus and the whore of Babylon, praying to the hand and not knowing if I'm supposed to save her or stone her, under the weight of all them wasted years, under vodka and coke, praying to the hand to show me.

MARK

It was so black in Cynthia's room when I woke it was hard to tell what was a dream and what was just black bedroom, and she said, "How darling," in a dream or not a dream, and later, in sleep or right after sleep, "It's your baby, if that's what you want to know," and later still, in another dream or not a dream, "It's his baby, if that's what you think will make a difference." There was no green aura indicating the presence of an apparition. I looked and listened and couldn't see or hear anything.

Dizziness and my skull shrinking over my brain waited until I opened the bedroom door, then hit all at once. I made it to the bathroom and closed the door on the day behind me, and after the tub filled, I sank into the hot water, imagining myself melting from my bones, shivering from the heat of it, my bones exposed, and then my rubbery skin regenerating over my skeleton. I rose from the water and dripped through the living room, dripped through the kitchen, the floors a mess, covered with dirt from the broken plant and the contents of emptied drawers. The place would never be the same, but I washed the walls and vacuumed the carpets, mopped the kitchen floor and put everything where I thought it belonged.

I took some of Cynthia's books and headed back to Garden City, the construction on the LIE by LeFrak City stopping traffic dead. I sat stuck in it a long time. My phone rang, but I didn't answer. It was Liz again, my ex-girlfriend. She left another message, asking me to call back. Traffic didn't move. I called work, even though I had the week off. Work was getting along fine without me. I was told to take another week, as much time as I needed. I didn't think there was that much. I sat in traffic, watching heat and exhaust shimmer off the asphalt in waves, distorting everything.

18

LIZ

The problem was he became a moralist, or just delusional, pretending he could walk away from the business of power and politics untouched, as though he hadn't been an alderman's staffer
when we met and fell so hard for each other. He was plugged
into the Cook County machine and I worked for a state senator,
David Lambert, who was eying a congressional seat on the north
shore, a safe seat the three of us talked about constantly, practically dreaming that race into existence, until Lambert hired
Mark for research and polling and officially launched the campaign. People thought we were crazy to go after a popular incumbent like we did, and maybe we were crazy—we certainly
didn't lack for confidence—but we also knew how strong Lambert was on the stump. He lit up every room he walked into. We
knew how he polled with women, especially regarding his posi-
tions on the lake and public schools and corruption in Spring-
field and Washington. He made people believe change was possible, and he swung a lot of votes. But it was Mark who clinched
the thing, uncovering dirt in the incumbent's payroll, kickbacks
and ghost employees and other sleaze, then dribbling it out with
no fingerprints to an increasingly rabid press. This is what I
mean about the babe in the woods routine that came up later. We

were pragmatists, for Christ's sake, bound by a tough political fight.

Lambert won with a quarter point margin, two years before Gore's debacle in Florida. We'd never seen the drama of a close election and we were drunk with it. After two recounts, I went to DC as Chief of Staff, while Mark handled constituent services back in Winnetka. This should have been our happiest time—we'd won against long odds, had established ourselves as potent, fresh blood—and we *were* happy. But once we discovered Lambert's little problem, everything between us started to crumble.

Before the campaign, during the campaign, after the campaign, Lambert had been fucking some seventeen-year-old from New Trier, Kara Tomlinson, though he claimed he didn't know she was a high school student. And, of course, she got pregnant. It fell to Mark to take care of the problem, a nasty job, certainly, so do it and get it over with. He had to make sure she got the abortion—pay for it, drive her, whatever—but also make sure she kept her mouth shut. He had to dig up dirt on her father, who was head of oncology at Rush, and convince her of Daddy's pending fall from grace, the destruction of her parents' marriage, her family, I don't know what all. She had to understand this was all scary and serious, but also just a stage of life, really, a part of growing up, almost typical. He had to show her the reality and make a trade. You got dirt. We got dirt. Let's work together to keep it buried.

This is when he changed. His mother's dying at home—and I felt so much for him then, because it was absolutely awful—but he couldn't box up Lambert's problem. He solved it, but he couldn't let it go. I gave him space. I knew it was nasty. Maybe we had been true believers at one time. Maybe it was hard to see something so base in Lambert, so stupid. But we were veterans by then, grownups working to further the ideals we'd cultivated and fought for. I mean, whether you *believe* in it or not, whether you *like* it or not, the political fight's going on, the scratching and kicking and clawing, and you can either be part of it, or you can retreat to your little Buddhist oblivion and get steamrolled. He was like a convert to veganism after six years slaughtering hogs, complaining about the pork grease he couldn't wash off.

He landed a job with Dunning and Wright in New York, a propaganda machine that swung voter referenda and other ballot initiatives, furthering the agendas of the moneyed interests. I loved him, but I couldn't stay with a man who was afraid to get his hands dirty for the greater good. And he couldn't stay with me because I was in it up to my elbows. I had a feeling he'd be back though. Maybe just a hope. He was so good at the game, and I knew he had ideals he'd fight like hell for, part of what I loved in him.

When Kara contacted us again, looking for another payoff, I thought she might provide the chance he needed. I told her Mark would be in touch, but he refused to return my calls. I tried for weeks to throw him a lifeline, calling over and over, but he wouldn't get back to me. He knew I wouldn't wait forever. The girl would talk eventually, and once she did, Lambert would confess to everything. My job was to save him from himself, to save them both, maybe. And what I said to Mark in my mind, in his ongoing silence: You want to be a moralist? Lend a hand to somebody fighting the good fight—answer your goddamn phone and let's finish what we started.

MARK

I sat in traffic surrounded by people going to work, imagining Cynthia and Kyle and the baby ghost floating through space, weightless, holding hands, never growing older, and I wondered what age would be ideal for death if that's how you'd spend eternity—floating through space like an amoeba in the ocean. I thought of my mother drifting among planets and space debris, then remembered her fear of flying, how she took sedatives and finally gave up on airplanes altogether when I was six or seven. "They turn them on," she said, "and never turn them off. Until they crash and turn themselves off."

She and I took the train from Chicago to Seattle when I was in second grade to visit her closest friend, Peggy Lynch, who didn't have a husband or kids, but did have a house full of candy I was allowed to gorge on. I slept with my mother on the train going out and in the big guest bed once we arrived, which was probably the best part of the trip—waking to her in bed beside me. On our last morning in Seattle, I got sick with a high fever, and all the way back to Chicago I came in and out of fevered consciousness as the country unrolled out the window beside my narrow bed, my mother there when I woke, feeding me chalky orange children's aspirin, feeding me ginger ale through a straw, feeding me chips of ice, placing a damp cloth against my forehead, her cool hand feathering my prickly scalp, her eyes looking down on me with adoration.

I wanted that fever and train trip to last forever.

NIKKI

The train into the city feels like a dry run for our escape, even though we have nothing with us and I worry that Celia's already changed the locks to Kyle's loft down on Broome Street. Alina seems lighter beside me on the subway downtown, excited as she always is to be in the city, as if the two of us are taking a break from our lives to go on this adventure, which in a way, I think, we are. She's only been to Kyle's place once, which makes me feel overprotective and stupid. Stupid, too, to think I'll find anything of value to sell, to steal. We take the freight elevator to the top floor, then walk the dark hallway to his door, Alina hushed and shrinking, and I wonder at my stupidity, bringing her here when the evidence of his life will only remind her of his absence, which I'm feeling now too, away from Long Beach and the possibility of Burke finding us, because he'd never find us at Kyle's place, and for just a second I think maybe we'll settle here for a few days.

I open the door and light pours into the hallway. Alina walks in like she owns the place, but is stopped by the paintings of me propped against Kyle's work tables. The entire space is given over to painting, except for the little kitchen and platform bedroom way in the back corner, the wide plank floors speckled with paint, and rough wood tables pushed against the walls. Skulls and doll heads and tin toys and flower pots and books and silk flowers and magazines cover every surface. Two assembled skeletons, one human, one bear, stand guard in their corners.

"This looks so much like you," Alina says, looking at a painting of me hung on the one clear wall, Kyle's work space. "But then it doesn't," she says.

"Right," I say, looking at Cynthia's eyes.

"I like these better than the one he gave us."

She opens the door to the rooftop deck and walks outside, leaving me staring at myself in oils, all the reds in these paintings, all my arrogance, based on nothing, captured perfectly, and I wonder how I could have been so distant from him. I flip through the canvases, some of me, some of Cynthia, and I feel so awful, not so much from the loss, but from how I kept myself removed from him, denying myself the possibility of loss. If I wouldn't or couldn't love him right, what had I been doing with him in the first place?

I'd take off my clothes in this place and remove myself from myself as he painted me, music filling the studio I would lose myself in, drinking a glass of wine as Kyle memorialized me, part of me thinking I deserved to be transformed into an object of beauty, another part of me understanding that the object had nothing to do with me, propped on his 1940's sheet-covered divan listening to Lucinda Williams or Luscious Jackson while he turned me into an abstraction. I didn't think he deserved this expensive loft in Soho, which I thought should belong to an already successful artist—not someone on the verge of possible success, not someone who hadn't earned the money it would take to live and work in a place like this, full of props and toys. I resented his trust fund money and this beautiful place his wealth had gotten him, never smart enough to see that smallness in myself, never trying to overcome such small sickness.

I climb the ladder to his sleeping platform above the tiny, useless kitchen and smell his sheets, the brick walls covered with photos of me and Cynthia and famous painters and women I don't know.

Alina walks in below and sits on a gray stool at one of his work tables. She picks up a skull and holds it away from herself, up toward the window, tears coming down her face but silent. I was only a little older than her when I ran out into the world, thinking I was finally free to become something other than my mother's nurse, so full of anger and life and unable to separate the two. She puts down the skull and picks up a dented copper pot, puts that down and picks up a flat, jointed, little wooden man, swinging it so his legs and arms spin.

"Hey," I call down.

She looks up at me startled, puts the little man back on the table.

"You can have that," I say, and Alina says, "It's not yours to give."

"He'd want you to have it," I say, climbing down the ladder.

"You don't know that," she says.

I was a fool to think we could stay here, with his and Cynthia's presence saturating everything. A fool to think I'd find anything to sell. I just need to call Mark and see if he can help us. But something holds me back. When I was 17 and penniless in Providence, I did practically anything for money. To survive. I had no problem with the implied exchange of sex for food or a place to stay. I had no problem stealing. And this isn't any different, even if I am so much older. Even if I do have Alina now. Because her survival is as important, more important, than mine then or now. Anyone would do anything to protect her child.

Maybe coming here is just a way of saying goodbye.

I rummage through a few drawers and cabinets, as though I'll find money or bags of gold, Alina over my shoulder asking what I'm looking for.

"My stuff," I tell her.

If Mark can't or won't get the money, we'll hit the road in the morning, or I'll put her with a friend while I handle Burke. But what will I tell her? I can't just park her at a friend's house so close to home. Or maybe I can. And I know Mark will help, if he can. Just the way he looked at me. Just because he has to. Just because we're in the middle of all this together. The only question is what words to use, though words don't always matter so much if something happens between people.

ALINA

You can see the twin towers from his rooftop deck poking over the squat wooden water towers on the roofs around us, old fashioned water towers like for trains in the wild west, except rising over rooftops. Mom's back inside with the paintings he made of her, naked and red and sort of empty or tired and way too sexual, always falling back on her body like she does. He probably would have painted me, too, not like that, not without clothes on, but I do have a sketch he made of me down on the beach that looks exactly like me, except a little prettier maybe—not the way you would ever see yourself, but more the way he saw me, probably. I knew he was sketching me that day because he kept looking over his sketchpad as I read in a beach chair, pretending I didn't notice and acting surprised when he gave me the drawing, which I love as my most cherished possession. It's on the wall over my desk back at Interlochen, which makes me wonder how I'm ever going to get my stuff, and I sort of panic for a minute and forget why I'm so sad and dead feeling, but then I don't care, because I remember he's gone forever, and then I do care, because that picture he drew of me is all I'm ever going to have of him.

On a clear day, you can see the twin towers from the bay side of Long Beach, which makes me wonder if we were ever looking at them at the same time, him on his deck here in the city and me back in Long Beach, riding my bike home from Magnolia Pier with Ashley. It's only my head in the sketch he made, and you can see every single hair, but he made another one, too—of me and my mother—that he drew from a photo she gave him. She has her arm around me on our front porch and we're smiling and look exactly like ourselves. Except happy, because nothing like this had happened to us yet.

I can hear her moving around inside, but when I walk through the sliding door from the deck, she's gone. It's such a huge cluttered space, she could almost blend into the paintings of herself or the skeletons in the corners or these big stuffed birds hanging from the ceiling among Chinese looking strips of long colored cloth fluttering. So much of him is here, it doesn't seem possible he won't just appear.

But this is a museum now. I hope it can stay like this forever, so I can come here when I want to be close to him, but they'll never let me do that, I'm sure. Maybe his mother would like me more than she likes my mom though, because of how much I really love him. Maybe she'll want me to be almost like a daughter to her, almost like a replacement for him, once she sees that I'm not at all like my mother.

I sit at one of his long work tables and pick things up he held in his hands.

My mother calls to me from a place I didn't know was here, hidden down at the end of the room on a platform up near the ceiling. She wants me to take something of his that isn't hers to give, a little wooden man. I hear her rustling as she comes down from the platform, and I put the wooden man in my pocketbook, not because she said I could, but because I knew I would all along.

She's beautiful in the paintings around me and kind of haunted in some it seems, or private, like he found something in her and showed it to the world, something she would have never shown herself. Something kind of lonely. Something private and kind of fierce and a little afraid maybe, but mostly strong and lonely.

Then she's right beside me holding a green toothbrush.

"Did you take that little man?" she says.

She pets my hair and I jerk away.

But she's been crying, her face washed out, nothing at all like in the paintings.

"Why do you have a toothbrush?" I ask her, and she looks down at it, and says, "It's mine."

"Why don't we stay here?" I say.

"We can stay as long as you like."

"Forever," I say.

"Alina," she says.

Like I'm just a stupid kid.

BURKE

I wake up weak and wobbly and have to get out of this place. I call Cinnamon from the payphone and get her goddamn machine again and think that every one of them's just exactly the same, all whores of Babylon trying to tear a man down. I swallow an oxycontin with my coffee, watching the whores in the coffee shop, young and old, all of them with secret whores inside them, and then while I'm looking at the comics and sort of brooding, the oxycontin smoothing everything out and bringing me back to normal, I get another revelation from Carl.

And it's this: Ain't no such thing as a pure, true victim. Victims make themselves victims, somehow want to be victims or done something that makes them deserve to be victims. Like Cinnamon not taking my calls. Or, worse, me all weak and weepy over Nikki, giving her the upper hand and making myself a victim. That's what hits hardest. How I'm letting her turn the tables on me, when it's her that killed Cash and ruined my family. Her that wants to be a victim.

It's a just God in a just universe, Carl always said, everything happens for a reason, but sometimes we can't see the whole picture and can't understand the justice that's being handed down. And if we get in the way of the hand, it'll reach out and crush us. To make yourself a victim is the greatest weakness and greatest sin, the reason the Jews was all gassed and burned, because none of them stood up to Hitler. But how could one man stand up against all that power? I asked him. Most couldn't, he said. Only a man who hasn't made himself a victim—a man strong enough and righteous enough to never really be imprisoned, no matter where he is—only that man can become a true, pure instrument of the hand, because the hand wouldn't take up with victims. It might make victims, but those people are weak and aren't really victims because they want to be victims. It's a matter of being strong in your mind, taking control of your life, and punishing those that deserve to be punished. Teaching them. Making them pure as you. A victim can only be a victim if she deserves to be a victim, which the guiding hand always determines.

That's when I feel the universe start to align again, me pushing my weakness away and deciding to test it by calling Cinnamon, having pure faith she'll answer, which of course she does, so happy to hear from me. We make plans for the evening, and I'm perfectly fine now—right and aligned—her all sweet and playful and apologetic about missing my calls, telling me she called too, over at the Royalty, and that she's looking forward to seeing me again, too, just a hint of the whore in her now, but in a good way. I tell her I want to take her out for dinner, and she says she knows a good place, but it's kind of expensive, asking my permission more or less, which I give her. At the mall buying new clothes for our date, I feel myself growing stronger and stronger, Cinnamon and me better than Nikki and Cash ever was, all these shoppers and me among them, a pure true instrument of the hand.

19

MARK

Everyone had called and left messages during my one day absence, including my father and sisters and friends and work and Denys and Nikki and Cynthia. No, not Cynthia. Cynthia was dead. The people who'd called, the living, were all sorry and wondering how I was doing. Nikki wanted me to call her back—she sounded a little drunk, with PJ Harvey playing in the background—but I was afraid to call her back. I didn't know if she was better off knowing what she knew or better off not knowing what she knew. It didn't seem likely that anything I'd learned would make much difference to her—Cynthia and Kyle's dead baby, if it was their baby—but maybe it would, and maybe it would only hurt her. She didn't seem capable of being hurt, though, a horrible, dehumanizing thought. Of course she was capable of being hurt. Everybody was capable of being hurt. And then I wondered how to hurt her, and thought it best if we never talked again.

Cards pushed through the mail slot lay in a scattered pile in the hallway, offering condolences. The phone rang and I was sure it was Nikki, hoping it was and hoping it wasn't. And then I thought it was probably Cynthia. But it was Cynthia's sister, Beth, calling to ask how I was doing.

"Not very well," I told her.

"Me, neither," she said.

"For one crazy second, I thought you were her on the phone," I said.

"I know," Beth said. "I do that, too."

"Like she's lingering," I said, and Beth said, "Exactly."

"Did you know she was pregnant?" I said

"Yes," Beth said. "But I didn't know if you knew yet."

"Of course I knew," I said. "But then, lately, these last couple days or hours, I've been confused about it, like questioning it. Like maybe it isn't even true."

A silence hung between us.

"Like maybe it's just a dream," I said.

"A dream?"

"Yes."

"I was with her when she took the test," Beth said. "It wasn't a dream."

"What was it?"

"She was pregnant."

"What else?" I said

"What else what?"

"What else did she say about it?

"Just—. How happy she knew you'd both be."

"Yes," I said. "Anyone would have been."

"It's so awful," Beth said.

"I have to go," I said, and I hung up the phone, knowing what I already knew. Knowing it even more.

It rang again a few minutes later, and I was certain it was Nikki. Okay, I thought, she has a right to know everything. But it was Liz, who I hadn't talked to in months. She'd left a million messages, and now she was calling twice in one day. I picked up and she told me she'd learned about the accident through my sister, and how sorry she was. I knew Liz would do whatever she could to help. Probably. I also knew she wanted something I wasn't going to give her.

Before she could bring up Kara Tomlinson, I told her about Cynthia's baby, everything spilling out of me.

"Slow down," she kept saying. "Take a breath."

"It wasn't mine," I said.

"Okay," she said. "But still."

I didn't have the heart to tell her I was practically unemployed. We'd shared so much love and focus and commitment—so much work and love and work all mixed together—that my disengagement from my current job would be incomprehensible to her.

She told me she'd do whatever she could.

One hand washes the other, I thought.

She told me she loved me.

I told her I loved her too, then hung up before she could bring up Kara and whatever they wanted me to do. I was done with all that.

She called again and I ignored her. She called several more times, before giving up. If Liz had been somebody else, we would have gotten married and had kids and taken them to Cubs games. I would have left the lying life of politics and done something different, though what that might have been was unclear since I didn't possess any skills, except lying. Maybe there was a good kind of lying you could do, some kind of charity lying, a job in the God industry. I didn't know who Liz would be if she were somebody else. Certainly not Cynthia. And I didn't know what role I could play in the God industry. Liz had thought it was the business with Kara Tomlinson that made me quit Lambert, and it was a little, but watching my mother die over those long months had made me hungry for something I couldn't name. I was too afraid to think I was wasting my entire life, so I ran to New York and Cynthia without much reflection. If Cynthia had been somebody else, we would have had kids and taken them to Mets games and hosted charity barbeques. Maybe we would have found something worth fighting to save.

"Our baby," Cynthia would have said.

"Oh, please," I said. "Your baby. Kyle's baby."

"Anybody's baby."

"Exactly."

KARA

Our first meeting was at the Original Pancake House in Wilmette, the place packed with families and hungover frat boys and Mark all shy and misty. When he asked what I planned to do, I looked at my melon bowl and cottage cheese and brought out one tear and then another, like in that Nirvana song when Kurt Cobain says, "The greatest day that I ever had, was when I learned to cry on command," and I didn't say anything, Mark like, "It's going to be okay," handing me a bandana from his pocket, as if I'm going to touch my face with that thing. I'd known before, but now I really knew how scared David was, just because of this Mark dude, obviously some power guy, waiting for me to stop crying—not that I would ever have hurt David. But they must have been crazy to read me as some teenage sex victim. As if I were Jerry Springer material. As if any of it!

With David and me, I was just so flattered at first. We'd drink champagne at the Drake, the lake huge out his window across Lake Shore Drive, and I'd feel so glamorous and sophisticated and not at all out of place—not once I got over the fact that this guy with so much to lose was investing his entire future in me, especially after he moved to DC. When I told him on the phone I was pregnant, I wasn't looking for anything—I was already completely in love with him, and just wanted him to know about the baby. But he freaked out, that dude Mark calling not ten minutes later to set up a breakfast meeting after my Saturday dance class. And all I could think was, Do you really think I'm this cheap and trashy? And, okay, if I'm nothing more than a lay to you, you're nothing more than a lay to me, too. So what?

We sat at the Original Pancake House, then drove to the lake and walked, Mark outlining *options*, the payoff. Of course he'd pay for the *procedure*, but he'd also provide something extra for my time, something for college, say 10,000? The whole thing was like a soap opera, and I was like, "I just want to think about this a little more."

The threats came a week later, sort of indirect and irrelevant. As if I didn't know my father was cheating on my mother. But then David and I started talking again—really talking—and we fell deeper in love, which was why I didn't understand Mark's tone when we met again the next week at the Skokie Lagoons.

"You can do whatever you want," he said. "But there's a hard way and an easy way, that's all I'm saying."

I knew how unhappy David was in his marriage. We were talking on the phone every night, growing closer and closer. And it was like Mark hadn't gotten the memo.

"How does Jenny feel about all this?" I asked him.

"Is that how you want to play it?" he said. "Ruin the man's life?"

We were walking toward the water, Mark giving off his thug vibe, the role he'd been cultivating since threatening to smear my dad in the newspapers. I wondered if he had a briefcase full of money in the trunk of his car. Or a gun.

"Doesn't he deserve to be happy?" I said.

"We're talking about what you deserve," Mark said.

That's when I knew someone else was pulling the strings, Mark probably. Because David was always available when I called now and we'd talk into the night, just about everything, and maybe it was the hormones or whatever, but I was starting to understand how unhappy he really was, how stressed he was in his work, how he wanted another life, and me, stupid, actually sort of believed him.

"What do I deserve?" I asked Mark, and that's when I got scared. It wasn't quite the way he looked at me—this squinty appraisal—more just the words themselves bringing up a mental image of my body crumpled in a dumpster somewhere.

"I'm not convinced it's what he wants," I said. "He wants another life," I said.

"You want to ruin his career?" Mark said. "And all the good he's trying to do?"

Two men in lawn chairs sat fishing by the launch ramp. A band of retarded adults wandered around a picnic blanket on the lawn. Kayaks and canoes skimmed across the water. "I know he's not happy," I said. "He talks about another life."

Mark dialed his phone and said, "She needs to know exactly what you want. Stop torturing her." He handed it to me.

"Are you busy?" I said, and David said, "Not at all. What's up?"

I waved Mark away and walked toward the water. I'd been so sure that day at the Original Pancake House, but all my talks with David had made me realize that nothing has to be inevitable. "So you want me to do this?" I said, and he said, "I want you to do what's best for you," and I said, "Is this what you want me to do?"

"If it's right for you, yes."

"What if it's not right for me?"

I was just trying to push him back to how we were on the phone at night or how we'd been in our suite at the Drake. His silence told me everything, and I felt so stupid then, as if I'd ever want a baby in the first place.

"I'll support whatever you decide," he said, but I knew he'd become a puppet, saying the same phrases over and over when you pulled the string on his back. That's what really scared me. How he wasn't even human anymore.

I turned and Mark was beside me. I handed him the phone.

If David had told me to drop everything and come to DC, get an abortion or don't get an abortion, I would have done it. That's what I regret, I guess, or what's so hard to get over—just how much I opened myself to him. And once I understood he didn't want me, I felt so stupid for ever having considered keeping it. If he'd just been honest with me, I never would have sunk into any feeling of possibility, not that I didn't shake the whole thing off immediately.

After Mark made the final offer—fifty thousand—he mentioned my brother Danny selling coke at Amherst, how far he'd fall, and I knew then that Mark could figure out anything, could track down dirt on anyone and destroy them. I was just so tired of the whole stupid game and never would have said a word about it to anyone, whether they paid me or not, but I took the money and spent every goddamn dime of it and never felt another thing about any of it except disgust. Then I wanted just a little more, ten thousand maybe, or twenty, but Mark's phone was disconnected and some bitch in David's office passed me off to some other bitch who said she'd track him down. He'd be in touch, she said. But he didn't get in touch.

I imagined him out in the world somewhere, killing people and paying people, and then I remembered how cow-eyed he was that day at the Original Pancake House and I didn't know which version of him was true. It's not that I regret my decision—far from it. But once the money was gone, I was like, Okay, what do I really have here?

DAVID

You think you'll never stop looking over your shoulder, knowing it might be revealed at any moment, hobbling you for the rest of your political life, if not destroying you. But time passes and you realize that what's buried might stay buried. I punished myself for months, struggled to understand how love blooms. Good luck can go to your head, I know that much. You start to believe the press. We never should have beaten Thompson in '98—the odds were too long—but we did. You start to believe in your own mythology, your own invincibility. And then you realize the hubris, fear finally infecting you once it becomes all too apparent what damage that kind of scandal can do. All that's left then is the hope that you can bury it deep enough that it never sees light again.

Her skin was flawless, her face radiant. She had the most beautiful body I'd ever seen, a dancer's body. We'd spend hours at the Drake during my recounts, Clinton's impeachment hearing on TV in the background. This is what I mean by hubris. She was only sixteen, a junior in high school, though I would have guessed she was twenty. Liz knew nothing about it. I would sneak away. Mark didn't know. It was just the two of us—becoming one. That might sound trite or clichéd, but it's just a limitation of the language, because there is no language for what our bodies knew, our souls. My recount was certified after Clinton's impeachment, two days before Kara's birthday. That's when I learned she was sixteen when things had started. I love my wife, my children. I thought a lot about Clinton's risk-taking behavior, identified with it completely. I knew what a fool I was.

You've never seen skin this warm and smooth, this electric to your touch. I was only 34, twice her age, yes, but just barely. I never doubted her when she said she was pregnant, never thought she was playing me. It broke my heart to turn my back on her emotionally, though in many ways I was more available to her those last few weeks than at any other time in our relationship. But she was as good as dead to me. There's no other way to say it. That was the horrible part. That and Mark's silent judgement, as if I were a monster. I would have kept that baby, raised that baby, sacrificed everything for that baby if that's what Kara had wanted, something Mark and Liz never understood. They could only consider the punishment I deserved, the punishment Kara deserved. I respect Mark's intelligence, his integrity, but I also believe he's sacrificed some part of himself to his ambition. He was devastated that I couldn't live up to what he'd made of me, what he wanted me to be. He was like a child, breaking what he'd once loved. I told him I was sorry. I offered to go public. Neither of them would hear it. This is what I mean by ambition. This is what I mean when I say that once someone wants a piece of you, wants to believe in you and live through you, that they die inside. Liz got over it. Mark didn't. It was his inability to forgive that destroyed him. And too much investment in me.

I've wept for the baby countless times, for the pain I put Kara through. I supported her as best I could, tried to help with the weight of her pain. I've carried it for several years. I carry it every day. But if you're going to move forward in life, you finally have to forgive yourself. You have to give yourself permission to be human. You have to learn that in order to give love, you must open your heart to the possibility of receiving love. I long for her still, for who she was and who we were together. In some ways, what we had never ends, even though I'll never see her again. It wouldn't be fair to her or to me or to my family. If that's hypocrisy, I'll cop to it. But I believe our love was first and foremost a celebration of life, a kind of prayer. At the end of the day, I'll have what exists between us in my heart forever. So will she. Mark couldn't understand the power of that kind of love. Liz couldn't. Their selfish ambition and ass-covering finally for them transcended everything, as if they'd closed their hearts permanently to the possibility of giving and receiving love.

20

MARK

The phone rang, but I didn't want to talk to anyone, until I heard Nikki on the machine, the sound of her voice like a shot of adrenalin, but calming too.

I picked up and she wondered how I was doing.

I told her I didn't know how I was doing, and wondered how she was doing.

She didn't know how she was doing either.

We met at a bar in Rockville Center, where she walked in wearing a summer dress, completely put back together since I'd seen her at the funeral home. We ordered drinks and she told me about her job selling ads for the *Long Island Weekly* and I told her about my propaganda work for Dunning and Wright, convincing voters to support deregulated electricity or Indian gambling or whatever concept we'd been hired to sell—that PCBs were safer left in riverbeds, for instance, or that universal health care would actually hurt everyone. Before my current job, I told her, I'd worked for a congressman, and before that an alderman, but I was done with all that now. We talked for a long time, leaning into each other, and she finally said, "Are you okay?"

I thought about Cynthia's baby and Cynthia lingering. "Not really," I said. "It's a long story."

"I've got time," she said.

"It involves you," I said, and she said, "Now you have to tell me."

The waiter came by to see if we wanted more drinks.

Nikki and I looked at each other. I kept breathing the air around us, trying to take her in. I asked her if she wanted to go somewhere else for a drink, and she did, but then we decided she should follow me to Garden City instead. I wasn't sure what we were doing. I wasn't sure what I'd tell her. I pulled into a liquor store, Nikki following, and we bought a bottle of tequila. There was an hour of light left, but it was cooling. We'd sit out back with the tequila and I'd tell her about Cynthia and Kyle's baby— if it was their baby—and Kyle's voice on the machine. But that all seemed so long ago and fading. Boring, really. Meaningless. What mattered now was just—

NIKKI

I told Alina Mark called *me*, all broken up, and that we were going to meet to talk about Cynthia and Kyle, to share our grief.

"So I *can* go to Ashley's?" she said.

"But not for a sleepover," I said. "It's a school night."

"Not for me," Alina said. "Ashely wants me to go to school with her tomorrow, anyway. And her mother said—"

"We'll see," I said, thinking I'd have to pick her up late if everything went right. I didn't know how Ashley's mother would feel about that, but when I called, she said it would be fine if Alina spent the night; or if I wanted to pick her up late, that would be fine, too. She understood. She wanted to help.

After I showered, Alina sat waiting in the living room with a backpack I knew she'd filled for a sleepover. I drove her to Ashley's and told her I'd pick her up later.

"How much later?" she asked.

"I'm not sure."

"This is like a date, isn't it?"

"No," I said.

"Right," she said, and she slammed the car door.

I went home and made phone calls while I dressed. I'd managed to gather around ten thousand dollars from friends and another five from my boss at the paper. He didn't know Kyle, didn't know I'd never need a loan for funeral expenses. Maybe fifteen thousand would be enough for Burke—at least to start. But that was a ridiculous thought. I'd never be through with him. Still, maybe I could convince him to leave us alone, pay him for his loss, somehow make him understand that I hadn't meant to hurt his brother. I thought again about calling the cops. Or maybe I'd take the fifteen grand and hit the road. But I'd never get far enough. I had to push it all out of my mind for the moment, had to keep pushing it out of my mind with Mark, which was easier than I thought it would be, the two of us talking, exchanging information about our lives, Cynthia and Kyle disappearing as he tells me about his career in politics and his current hideous job. This guy is even more connected than I thought he was. But he surprises me with his disgust for the life he's led, like he's been hurt by it more than those kind of people usually are. I lose track of time, Friday and what I want far away for minutes at a stretch, time almost stopping or creating seconds to breathe in.

I follow him to Garden City and it's like I'm already gone from here, every threat buried behind me. But Alina's behind me, of course. It's just a tease is all it is. Just a moment to rest in.

BURKE

We went to a fancy Italian place with oysters and wine and salad and some kind of pastry dessert and brandy and coffee, close to

400 bucks with the tip. It was all rich people there, but Cinnamon didn't look whorish, and I had on a shirt and tie and pleated pants I picked up at the mall. It felt like I was settling in to a new life—money and fancy dinners, a beautiful girl, all of it, just like Nikki and Cash. We went back to the Royalty, drunk and mellow and settled into each other, knowing what was going to happen next. I wondered what I could make her do with just my mind, how much of herself she'd surrender. I wondered if she was a pure, true victim.

I had no interest in hurting her. It was more a matter of getting my money's worth and playacting, thinking about the times Nikki and Cash had while I was rotting. I told her stories about me and Nikki so young and in love before they killed her. I asked what she thought I ought to do to the killers that took everything from me, what kind of justice I ought to lay down.

She looked at me a long time, sitting on my lap like she was. She held my face in her hands and fed me a bump of coke. "I think the only way to get over her," she said, "is to somehow set her free." She kissed my forehead, ran her hand through my hair. "I don't mean forget her," she said. "I'm not saying that at all. What I'm saying is to let it go, her and whoever hurt her."

"After everything they done?" I said.

"I know it's not easy," she said.

I kissed her, hating her for trying to poison me with weakness like she was, like Jesus and the whore of Babylon. She kissed me back, all sweet and whorish, and I realized she was falling in love with me—the reason she wanted me to forget Nikki in the first place, so she could have me for herself, wanting me to forget everything and make myself the victim. But that wasn't going to happen. Not now and not ever.

21

MARK

I put her on the patio and brought out beer and tequila and shot glasses and salt and a bowl of limes. "What about music?" she said.

I brought that out too, poured us shots.

"It's nice out here," she said, nodding toward my aunt's backyard enclosed by trees and shrubs and other plants. "I've never had a good yard for Alina."

I didn't know who Alina was, then remembered she was Nikki's daughter.

"She looks so much like you," I said, and Nikki told me about getting pregnant in Austin during high school, her boyfriend a bassist in some band I didn't know, and how he didn't care about the baby one way or the other. "I was living with my cousin," Nikki said, "my mom up in New Hampshire all crazy on the phone once I told her I was pregnant. And when I say crazy, I mean certifiably. I didn't really have anyone in the world, except my cousin, and I was like, I just want to know who this baby is. I was too young to be a mother maybe, but I was also like a thousand years old."

She told me about her dad dying in Vietnam before she was born and her mother's cancer and mental illness, her mother making Nikki do all kinds of crazy shit around the house. "I'm

twelve years old," she said, "setting off roach bombs in the kitch-
en. My mom's in the next room, saying the insecticide can't hurt
her after all the drugs they've pumped into her. But she'd make
me leave while the poison sprayed, and that became my escape
time."

She took a drink and pointed at the cigarettes on the table.
"Can I have one of those?" I handed her one and lit it. "Everything was so weird back then," she said. "I had this friend, Crystal, who loved music as much as I did. We developed this elab-
orate fantasy—I don't know how it evolved, exactly, but it was
hilarious. I would pose as Chrissie Hynde from the Pretenders,
and she would be Debbie Harry from Blondie, and on Saturdays,
when the roach bomb was going off, we'd shop in the thrift stores
for jewelry and dresses and jeans and tee shirts, all the stuff that
would transform us into these women we idolized. We'd only answer to their names with each other, like we were trying to burn
away everything in us that wasn't them. When I look back now,
the weird part is how my memories of that time—me at home
with my sick mother versus me with Crystal as a pretend woman
out in the world—how those memories don't align at all, how
they never overlap, like there are two lives back there for two different people, the girl at home and the fantasy girl. My mom was
disintegrating and I'd leave and pretend to be so tough, those two
girls never meeting even once."

She told me about running to Providence when she was 17,
the tough girl finally taking over completely, and how she had to
get even tougher, so poor and trying to survive, but how music
saved her or fed some softer part of herself. I told her I'd lived in
Providence around that time, too, just after she left, and we un-
covered all the ways our paths crossed outside of time in Providence, the places we had in common, Babes and the Living Room
and Lupo's, and the music, Sebadoh, Throwing Muses, the Pixies,
places we ate and drank, and the bands we almost saw together.

We leaned toward each other as we remembered the clubs and record stores, everything in Providence when we were so young, and it seemed like the world was shrinking, that we'd just missed each other and were finally finding each other. It seemed pointless to tell her about Cynthia and Kyle. They'd become irrelevant. She talked about washing dishes at La Chatte du Maison, the panhandlers she'd known on Thayer Street before she settled in. I couldn't stop looking at her, breathing the air around her.

"Let's do another shot," she said, "but a small one." She told me about moving to Austin, then Portland, on the run it seemed like. But when I asked her what from, she said it hadn't been a matter of running away, necessarily, more a matter of what she was moving toward. "And what was that?" I said, and she said, "I don't know. *You* probably," and she was smiling and sort of glowing, looking at me like whatever it was we were talking about, past, present, future, we were in it together, just like we'd almost been together all those years ago in Providence.

NIKKI

I tell him stories from my life, most of them true or mainly true, and it all feels so natural on this patio hidden from the world. When he goes in for more beer, I follow him and ask to see his music, which is a much better collection than I would have guessed. I pick out some discs and go back to the patio, putting on that Breeders EP, *Safari*, the second song, "Don't Call Home," playing when he comes back out.

"Come on," I say, standing and holding out a hand to him. "Let's dance."

I'm expecting resistance, but he takes my hand and we dance like a couple idiots, working up a sweat on his patio as the light fades.

Then he wants to pick a song. Then I do.

We do a spastic robot dance to Bowie's "Fashion," an under-water arm flapping dance to Beck's "Beercan," both of us laughing, taking each other's hands, letting go, and grabbing again. We dance and dance, pausing only for shots, and then he puts on "Summertime Rolls" and pulls me close and we're kissing, everything more blurry than I thought it would be. We sway to the music and keep kissing and then it's more than swaying, this hunger feeding itself, pushing and pulling, and we're down on the prickly grass in all this humidity, sweating against each other in the wet air like we're melting. We stop and rest and talk and start again. I catch myself looking at him looking at me, just the two of us here, like we're out in space, and I feel so close to him, his eyes on my eyes looking at me looking at him, and my eyes closing as he falls away and I fall away, and then later, when I start to surface from this emptiness, I'm surprised it happened this way, almost naturally, as though I hadn't planned it at all. As though I never wanted anything more.

We breathe for a minute on his lawn, the sky dull from the haze and light pollution. I run my hands up and down his back. It never gets dark enough here. I can hear a stream of traffic somewhere far away.

"And then you left Portland," he says, picking up our earlier conversation, as if nothing has happened.

I laugh.

"What?" he says.

"You were going to tell *me* a story," I say. "Remember? How it's about me too?"

We lie on our backs, our arms and shoulders stuck against each other. I put a leg over his leg.

"The whole thing's so crazy," he finally says, and he tells me about Kyle's pants, which he wants to show me, and I say, "I don't need to see them; I believe you," but he insists, bringing out a bag from which he takes a sheet to spread on the grass beneath us, and the leather pants, which he holds out to me, then stuffs back into the bag.

"I know they don't mean anything," he says.

He walks to the patio and grabs our beer, the cigarettes.

"That's not the story," he says. "Or maybe it is, kind of. I don't know. I'm not saying I'm happy she's dead." He offers me a cigarette.

"Of course not," I say.

"But I'm not exactly unhappy she's gone either. I mean—just from my life, which I know sounds horrible. It's just—all this unfinished business, all this crazy shit she set in motion. The money she came from and what that would have done, and how she never really understood what being rich meant. Not that I know what it means."

My antennae quiver at the mention of money, and I feel so cheap and hideous, as though I ever forgot what this was all about, except that when we were talking and dancing and then on the lawn all of that seemed far away, like I could just be with someone without some greedy, selfish motive driving everything. Like I could lose myself, which seems like the most selfish thing of all when I think of Alina.

"I discovered this stuff at her apartment," he says. "Kyle's pants and his voice on her machine setting up that night, but also, and this is the main thing: all this baby stuff, prenatal vitamins and a list of names and other stuff, and it just stopped me cold, freaked me out and sent me into this spiral. And I was like, There's no way this is true. But I called her sister, who confirmed that Cynthia was pregnant, and I'm sort of putting it together, but also—this is the weird part—I'm like, There's no way that baby's mine, somehow knowing it's Kyle's—"

And before I can stop myself, I say, "That's wrong. I'm sorry. But it wasn't his baby."

"I know you might want to believe that," he says. "None of this really matters."

"Listen," I say, knowing I shouldn't be telling him this, wanting to protect him, for Christ's sake, but also wanting to tell him the truth, thinking maybe he deserves that much. "Kyle had a vasectomy," I say. "Around ten years ago."

Mark hits his cigarette, looks away.

"I'm sorry," I say.

"It doesn't matter," he says.

"Maybe it does matter," I say. "I'm not saying it's for the best. But maybe that part does matter."

"I don't know why it would."

I kiss the side of his face, around his ear. He turns to me and we wrap ourselves around each other, as though we're regular people. As though anything like this could happen between us. As though I can help him. Because, the thing of it is, I want to.

He looks at me, runs his hand through my hair, and I'm wondering who the hell I am. I look at him but don't say anything. I reach up for another kiss and another, this hunger in me I can hardly remember feeling, except in my mind from way back, but not in my mouth like this, not in my throat, not in my stomach or legs or chest. I hold onto him because I want to look at him like before, I want him to look at me, just him and me floating in space, looking, and then I close my eyes because I want the blackness one more time, that complete surrender. But I can only have it a minute before I'm thinking I can't fall asleep when this is over. There's still so much to do, to say, not wanting to say it but knowing I have to, not knowing exactly what to say or how to say it, and then letting it slide for a minute, just a minute, just a few more minutes.

MARK

All I wanted was to touch her and listen to her and look at her.

Everything seemed perfect with her—talking and saying stupid things in these moments of rest, her saying, in a faraway voice, as if we'd been having this conversation for weeks or months or years, "But who do you think's the most disappointing solo artist—you know, really disappointing—after being in a great band?"

She looked down at me, her hair brushing my face, hanging around us.

"Of all time?" I said, and she said, "Yes, of all time," and I said, "Sting?" and she said, "Maybe," and I said, "But you have a better answer."

"Stevie Winwood," she said, and I said, "Oh, God. Right. What about Ringo?"

"But that's different," she said. "Because we expect so little from him."

"What about Mick?"

"I don't think his solo stuff really counts. I mean, the Stones are always still there. Whereas, with Traffic, Blind Faith. . . ."

"Okay, okay. Say something else."

"Like what."

"Anything."

She started moving again.

"What about Frank Black?" I said.

"No," she said. "Because he's good, even though the Pixies were better."

"Who was best then? In a great band, and even better as a solo artist?"

I pushed my fingertips against the pulse buttons in her neck.

"That might be harder," she said. "I don't think you can say Bob Marley. Because those first two Wailers albums are as good as anything he ever did."

"What about Elliott Smith?"

"But all his real stuff's solo."

"Ryan Adams?"

"Maybe. . . ."

"What about. . . ?"

"Yeah. . . ."

We stayed in the backyard for hours, and after all that time talking and not talking I felt like an idiot for bringing out Kyle's pants, but then it didn't matter. She told me about his vasectomy, which took me a minute to understand, because I'd been so sure of the story I'd constructed, Cynthia and Kyle's dead baby, my dead baby.

That news jolted me, the kid sort of rising, but then I felt relief that Cynthia was gone and the baby, too; because even if we hadn't stayed together, we would have been joined by that baby, and I could just imagine the arguments, especially with the trust fund money Cynthia would have smeared all over the kid, the snotty kindergarten and prep schools she'd have insisted upon, horseback riding lessons and country clubs. I felt liberated from all that horror, as if I'd just woken from a bad dream, and then guilty at my selfish relief, but feeling this creeping loss, too, making me wonder when I'd developed what must have been some kind of compassion or respect for life or whatever it was that felt like the loss of something I'd never had in the first place, this feeling like touching something beyond me or so much bigger than me, and Nikki there, pulling me back, something else that seemed impossible. Nikki.

I had to stop being so tiny and selfish and just be grateful for any time I could have with her. Not so petty and small and jealous and possessive of a dead person I didn't even want to be with, or a living person in the future—Nikki—already fearing what we'd do to each other, when we didn't even have each other and never would, whatever having someone could mean, but already afraid of what we'd turn each other into.

"She should have told you," Nikki said. "And I'm sure she would have."

"Maybe," I said. I couldn't shake or quite identify this hollowness, as though something had been taken from me, unable to tell if this loss could possibly be related to a dead baby I'd never even known about, then feeling like I had something to confess, some melodramatic role to fall into, wondering if Nikki herself might be pregnant already and hoping she was, sort of astonished by this person—myself—who suddenly seemed to want a kid and not trusting that at all . . . because it was nothing more than a romantic abstraction, an attempt to address an alien loss, or to fill something lacking, and wondering just where that came from, all these thoughts like an electrical storm flashing in my mind that I needed to put away somewhere.

We lay on a sheet in my aunt's backyard, Nikki against me breathing as the minutes unwound. We were quiet a long time, and I felt myself becoming entirely empty or full. Then she said, quietly, almost as if she didn't want to say it or didn't want me to listen, "Hey," and propped herself on an elbow looking at me.

"I don't know quite how to say this," she said. "But I need a little help with something."

"Okay," I said, sort of half asleep and waiting for whatever she was going to say.

She cleared her throat. "This is so embarrassing," she said.

I ran my hand up and down her back.

"I'm wondering about a loan," she finally said.

I felt the air seeping out of me. "Money?" I said.

"I'm sorry to bring this up," she said. "There's a timing issue, though. That's why. Oh, God. It's just—I didn't know this was going to happen with us."

Her skin against my skin, all the places our skin met. Sort of clammy and rubbery.

133

"How much" I said, sickening myself by calculating how much she might be worth. I had six grand in the bank.

"Thirty-five thousand," she said.

I laughed.

"It's not funny."

"It is," I said. "Why do you think I could come up with that kind of money."

"All those rich people at Friday's lunch. Cynthia's family. I don't know. There's no one else I can go to."

She was watching me closely, but she seemed patient, too. Like she could wait.

"What's it for?" I said, and she pulled away and sat up.

"I have to get Alina," she said.

"Okay," I said. "But when do you need this money?"

"Thursday," she said. "Late."

She started to dress. So did I.

"Two days?" I said.

"I have to get Alina," she said.

"I can't put my hands on that kind of cash that fast."

"I bet you can," she said.

"No, I can't," I said.

"But what about someone—"

"Impossible," I said, and we looked at each other and away. It seemed like there was nothing between us anymore and no way to get back whatever we'd had. We walked to her car, and she surprised me by kissing me out front on the driveway.

When she pulled away, she said, "I don't want you to think—"

"It doesn't matter what I think."

"—that I planned this or something. I didn't know this was going to happen between us."

"I'm not saying I don't want to help."

"It's just money."

"But I don't have it."

"This guy's coming after me," she said.

"What?"

"I have to get Alina," she said, a look on her face I hadn't seen before, sort of naked and vulnerable, almost pleading, but something else woven around it, too, toughness or control, like she was fighting with herself and not quite containing whatever she was trying to conceal.

"What guy?" I said, and she said, "I have to get Alina. We can talk tomorrow."

"What guy?" I said.

"Forget it," she said, and I said, "I want to know."

"Tomorrow," she said.

She kissed me again and I kissed her back. I watched her pull away.

Thirty-five grand wasn't the problem. The timing was the problem. And what if she took the money and ran, all her stories about running and whatever was chasing her that she wouldn't reveal—probably this asshole guy she'd mentioned. Liz would find a way to float the loan, as long as I took care of Kara Tomlinson, which I wasn't going to do. Because I was done with all that. I had another beer, wondering who Nikki owed and why. Maybe I'd help her even if she was going to run. I didn't want to believe every human interaction was nothing more than a transaction.

"You should help her because you can," my mother would have said. "Not because you expect something in return."

But I didn't think people worked that way.

Everyone wanted something—Cynthia and Liz and Nikki and Kara. But with Kara it had been so easy, finally. David Lambert wanted something. Then Kara wanted something. Then Lambert wanted something else. All of it finally resolved itself with money. But I could hardly believe Nikki was like the rest.

135

Maybe Cynthia had been right about babies being generators of something larger—the only good in this world, at least until they grew up. I poured another shot and toasted Cynthia and the dead baby. And Nikki. God. Nikki.

22

ALINA

When I was little she'd take me everywhere, to dinners and parties, and I'd sleep in some room and wake to her carrying me, pretending to sleep as she buckled me in, pretending to sleep all the way home so she'd have to unbuckle me and carry me inside, where I'd wake and ask if I could sleep with her, which she always let me do. But I'm too big for that now and I wouldn't want to be carried anyway.

I told Ashley about Kyle coming to Interlochen, how that was supposed to happen tomorrow, which she can't believe, until I make her believe, and then I confess that I was maybe even a little in love with him. She's seen him before, too, and she's like, "Oh, my God. Did your mom know he was coming?" And I'm like, "As if," and tell her how my mother was just using him for money for Interlochen, which we both think is so sick and typical. Ashley's mom and dad split up when she was little, and her mom got a fur coat from some guido almost immediately after her dad moved into the city, exactly like my mom already making a play for Cynthia's husband, or whoever he is, that Mark guy. We lay in her room talking late, my ears perking up at any car door slamming on the street, wishing I could just stay here forever.

"What did he look like?" Ashley asked. "When he was dead."

We'd been quiet a long time.

"The same," I said. "Sort of. I kissed him."

I started crying, because I should have kissed him—because they wouldn't let me do that and the casket was closed—but also because of everything. We talk a little more, before rolling over to sleep, but I can't sleep because I'm waiting.

Then she's rustling me in her beautiful blue dress, perfume around her, smoke and liquor, petting me and rubbing my back and up under my hair on my neck, the secret place she touches me, saying, "Come on, baby. We have to go home."

I roll over like I'm asleep. Like I'm four years old and need to be carried. But I don't want to be carried. I just want her to leave me alone. She pulls me up and half carries me downstairs into another hot night, puts me in the front seat and fills the car with her liquor and perfume smells. I keep my eyes closed tight, thinking, Kyle.

BURKE

"I don't do backdoor," Cinnamon says. "I told you that."

I've got her tied spread eagle on the bed, face down.

I've got some massage oil I've been rubbing into her skin, and a tube of lube I picked up at the pharmacy. I rub the oil over her shoulders, strong, but fragile, too, rub her long, golden back and down to her ass and up, then more lube on my fingertip, and she says it again, only a little sharper.

"I don't like that, Steve," she says, Steve being who she thinks I am.

When I don't answer, she tries to twist her head toward me, but she can't see a thing because my necktie's wrapped around her as a blindfold.

"Steve!" she says. More sharpness.

I massage the backs of her knees, her calves.

"Did you hear me?" she says.

"It's okay, Nikki," I whisper. "I heard you."

"I'm not Nikki," she says.

"Shh," I say, thinking, You're whoever I say you are.

Hating her for that denial.

I pour more oil in my hand, rub her thighs and hips, back up to her shoulders and down to her ass, all of it mine, and back up and down, kneading her ass, my hands slick with the oil.

"Come on," she says. "Let's do it."

"Shh," I say. "We will."

I keep rubbing, finding the movement she likes, the pressure, working my thumb up and circling and she clenches and says, "I told you, Steve. I don't do that," but I ignore her—she's tied down tight—working my thumb around—she starts to buck— "I'll scream, motherfucker," but she knows what she owes and I've been as gentle as can be and I push my thumb in and she screams and I hit her above her ear, hard, a sort of chopping blow, and tell her to shut the fuck up. All this massage oil, all this lube, it's not like I'm trying to dry fuck her.

"One more sound," I tell her, "and I'll kill you."

I could too, everything she's done to me.

I wrap my hands around her throat as I push against her.

"You gonna be quiet?" I whisper.

She nods.

"I don't want to hurt you unless I have to."

She nods.

"If you scream again, I'll kill you."

I let my hands loose, but I'm watchful, ready if she makes a sound.

"You need a little more lube down there?"

She nods.

"Now, isn't this nice," I say.

She nods, and I say, "Say it," and she says, "Yes."

It's the resistance that gets you in trouble, fighting the hand.

"I want you to feel yourself letting go," I tell her.

We're joined and she's given up fight, and I'm glad she's not going to make me hurt her, that she's finally and completely surrendered to my will. She's a smart girl, and beautiful. And I don't have a thing against whores. Just know your place is my way of thinking. Just pay what you owe.

23

KYLE

The best times on the beach are early morning or just before night, when time disappears, just you and your feet and the sand and the tide and Nikki and Alina and everyone sort of free for a minute as the light fades or comes on in the morning, the wind swirling and the waves unfolding, keeping their endless count, just you and the ones you love up against it, before anyone gets hurt yet or ever has, part of this gigantic movement, this beautiful dream, the beautiful empty enormity.

JESSICA

At first I was just happy to be alive, not even torn up, and it's probably an opportunity cost, but it's never happened to me before, not even close. Part of me wants to tell Armand, so he can track the motherfucker down and give him a serious beating or worse—not that there's a mark on me—and part of me wants my own revenge, tying him down and shoving a gun up *his* ass.

But you're *alive*, I keep telling myself, because for a long time I didn't think I was going to make it. Not just him clubbing me with his fist or choking me, pulling my head back by my hair. But the way he talked all the way through it, soothing me it felt like at the same time he was raping me, the necktie so tight around my eyes I couldn't see anything, not even at the edges. And how he talked after, rubbing my shoulders and down my back, making me swallow a pill, rubbing my throat like you would a dog's, making me hit from the vodka, still tied and blindfolded, and then slapping my ass, hard and then harder and then harder and harder until he started in on me again, whispering in my ear, "Gentle," and smearing lube all over me, "It's not gonna end 'til you cum, Nikki," rubbing me with oil and sticking it back in. I tried not to move the wrong way, certain he was going to kill me, Steve saying, "I can't hear you, Nikki." He wrapped his hands around my throat. "Should I, Nikki? Or shouldn't I?" and I tried to make the sounds he wanted, groaning, moaning, all these porn shit sounds, faking it as hard as I could, until he finally came and lay his dead weight on top of me for what felt like a long, long time.

"I ain't got AIDS," he whispered, "if that's what you're thinking."

He got off me and moved around the room.

I tried to focus on my breathing and nothing else. Just air filling my lungs.

"Everything's gonna be okay," he said. "You wanna drink?"

I shook my head, still blindfolded, still tied down.

"Come on," he said, and I said, "Okay," and he fed me more vodka, the liquor running down my face onto the bed.

"I'm gonna give you another oxycontin," he said, "to help you sleep."

I lay as still as I could, waiting for him to kill me, the lube drying as I tried to take myself out of my body tied to the bed.

"Open your mouth," he said.

He rubbed my gums with his finger, smearing what I hoped was crushed oxycontin and not poison around my mouth. I tried to spit it out, to dribble it as I heard him walk to the bathroom, praying he hadn't fed me enough for an overdose.

"You're a good girl," he said. "Smart. That's what I like."

I heard him pick something up. Put it down. A gun? A knife?

"I'm leaving twelve hundred on the table," he said. "That about right?"

He put his hand on my shoulder, rubbed the base of my neck.

"I'll be checking on you," he said. "I'll be back. I'm going to set this alarm so you know when to get up. Okay?"

I started to shiver.

"You all right?" He kept rubbing my neck, my skin waiting for him to clamp down and start choking. He pulled the blanket over me and that's when I thought he was going to shoot me in the head, standing over me like that, patting my back.

"You've got to settle down," he said, and then I thought he'd kill me if I didn't stop shaking, to make me stop. But I couldn't.

He got on the bed and wrapped his arms around my body still tied down.

"It's okay," he whispered.

He rubbed his hands over my back and ass and legs over the blanket, but that just made it worse, and I was trying so hard to stop.

"Look," he whispered. "You've got to stop this shaking."

"Maybe if you could get me some water," I said, because I thought if he just got off me I'd be able to stop.

"Just like a little kid," he said.

I heard the tap run in the bathroom. He put the cup to my mouth, but my head was turned sideways so that most of the water spilled onto the bed.

"That's just going to make you colder," he said. "Let me get another blanket."

I heard him at the closet. "Ain't one," he said. "But this bed-spread should do."

I felt another blanket cover me.

"Lie still and rest," he said. "You can get up when the alarm goes off, or maybe I'll be back before then. Maybe I'll be back in an hour or so. Or fifteen minutes. Maybe we'll go out for breakfast."

"Okay," I said.

"All right then," he said. And finally: "Goodnight now," and I said goodnight, and he kissed my cheek and stood somewhere above me, maybe trying to decide if he was going to kill me. I heard the door open and close and him walking away. And then I lay as still as I could for what felt like a long time, telling myself I was hardly even hurt at all if he didn't come back and kill me.

I thought I'd count to a thousand until I moved, wondering if he was maybe still there watching me. Distant sounds came from other parts of the building, a humming, a muffled shriek of laughter. I was certain nobody was in the room, but I kept counting, and each time I came close to my number, I added another hundred, starting to feel myself alive and really lucky, trying not to let other feelings come until I was safe out of there and could make a decision about how I was and what I should do.

The drugs made a cocoon around me, and I kept counting, remembering that guy killing girls a few years back, Joel something, all those girls he killed. I thought of Steve calling me Nikki and suddenly knew it was him that killed her, but then I wasn't sure. Because even though he was such a motherfucker, toying with my life like he did, he seemed careful all the way through not to hurt me. That made me hate him more than anything, as if he'd tried to steal a piece of my hatred. But then I thought of Nikki and how I could have ended up like her, or all the girls Joel what's his name killed, and I knew today wasn't just another day. I was *alive*. I tried to think of how I could hold onto that feeling and cherish my life and not take one more second for granted. The fucker. As if he'd given me that. But then I knew I'd given it to myself.

BURKE

Too many rodents is the problem, like Dallas or Houston, rats in a cage fighting and clawing and eating each other alive. Even at four in the morning, there's people crawling my ass to pass, racing to their heart attacks, while I toodle along, not letting them turn me into a rodent, innocent—and that's the thing of it—because I ain't done nothing. I'm sort of suspended between not doing nothing and doing it, looking forward to letting Cash rest, but at this moment just pure and clean, the air soft with the smell of day coming on, and my duffel in the trunk with my mother's gun, no way for a cop to gain access because there's nothing on me to warrant a look, no blood from Cinnamon because none was drawn. And it feels good to think of her future waiting to unfold—her life given back—while I drive into tomorrow. There's a freedom in it, too, driving when most everyone's asleep. Like you might be on your way to discover something, which, of course I am. Relief, too—that Cinnamon's still asleep, for instance, and that even if she does call the cops, there's no way for them to find me.

I drive around feeling my freedom, drinking coffee and smoking cigarettes, until the rodents get thick and I head back toward the city and a new motel, something near the airport where it won't raise suspicion to check in so early. Part of me regrets I won't be able to see Cinnamon after the business with Nikki gets put to rest. Then I wonder if maybe I can, her and me ending up on an island somewhere, having drinks on the sand, Cinnamon understanding it was all Nikki's fault, that I was tracking my brother's killer, Cinnamon forgiving me once she knows the whole story, me just sorry I couldn't tell the truth earlier: "But I didn't know you," I'd tell her. "That's why I couldn't tell it straight up from the start. And I'm sorry for what I done, even if I never hurt you and paid more than double and made you cum time and again."

I get sort of lost in my imagined conversation with her, driving in traffic so early on the Southern State Parkway toward Kennedy Airport and my next motel and a few hours rest. It's a good feeling, knowing what I gave her, knowing she's alive and has so much in front of her, babies and love and who knows what all. A sort of infinity there.

NIKKI

We don't have air conditioning, and even this close to the ocean it must be eighty degrees upstairs. Alina twitches and kicks and I keep waking, snatching pieces of dreams through tequila fog and my headache, though dreams have nothing to tell me. I was stupid to try to get money from Mark, stupid to sink into black emptiness with him, as though I deserved that escape. In my half sleep, I'm still deluding myself, still hoping he'll help us, when he has no reason to help after the way I treated him, the way I felt something between us and then clawed after money, betraying us both. Alina twitches and kicks, and I know how wrong I was to try to play him, when he seems like the only person I want to know besides Alina. Another delusion, the user part of me making me believe I could have feelings so fast.

A car door slams on the street, jerking me fully awake. I run to the window, but it's just Cathy Hayes coming home from the bars.

I get back in bed and drift into sleep. I wake in a panic, remembering my failure to kill Cash at Duval. What if I show the same weakness with Burke? What if he kills me and takes Alina and does what his brother did, and I'm like, that will never, because that can't ever—and that's when I know we're leaving in the morning. No more waiting. No more trying to find a way out. I can hardly believe how stupid I've been. We'll leave in the morning, even if we have to run forever. Sweat pops and cools on my forehead, runs in a line down my side. I concentrate on breathing, waiting for the relief of escape to settle over me.

She's so beautiful in her sleep, so peaceful, even when she twitches and kicks, as if her body knows there's a reason to run. Or maybe those are just my genes in her legs exercising themselves, priming her. I hope she won't have to run her whole life like I have. But at least she knows how. At least I gave her that. Besides, maybe running's all anyone does, until we finally get stopped or can't run anymore, everyone finally run down like a clock that can't be wound again.

Alina

I wake up early like when I was little, my mother snoring beside me, sleeping off whatever she did last night with Cynthia's boyfriend, liquor and cigarettes and sex and everything else. The whole room smells of it. She's so beautiful—even with her mouth open and her hair in tangles, the faint crow's feet and lines on her forehead smoothed out with sleep—and it makes me feel better, a little, to look at her asleep, even though today's the day he was supposed to come to Interlochen and now I'll never see him again, which I don't want to spiral into. But another part of me wants to hold onto that, not the loss, exactly, but just what he meant to me, which I'm not even sure what he did mean, except I was in love with him and shouldn't have been. Nobody knows that, though, except Ashley. I can hold that feeling to myself or take it to the beach and bury it. And even though his ashes would probably never find their way from the Sound all the way around the island and into the ocean, I can bury my part of him in the sand so that the same water his ashes are in might somehow wash over the part of him I have.

On the beach so early there are fishermen and old people walking and some yuppies jogging before work, but hardly anyone. Mist comes off the ocean, the city behind me, and it's not hot yet, the ocean loud and the wind blowing and old people walking dogs. I never understood how people could tell if the tide's coming or going just by looking at it, and I can't tell if it's coming or going now, but I walk on the hard sand below the high tide line, my hands wrapped around Kyle's wooden man in the pocket pouch of this poncho hoody he gave me from Guatemala. I walk toward the sun coming up way down the island toward Montauk, past the rich people in the Hamptons, and further out England and Ireland and France, where it's already night probably, and further still China and Japan, where it's another day entirely, and I think that's what being dead must be like—another day entirely.

I hold his wooden man in my pocket pouch like a mother kangaroo, walking him on the beach. Maybe his ashes floated around Manhattan and into the ocean drifting toward Long Beach, where I walk with this feeling of him in my hands.

That liquor smelled so awful coming from her, sour and sweet, filling her room. But she did cry yesterday at Kyle's, and also her mother dying and whoever my father was, and Kyle and how awful it would have been, really, if he had come to Interlochen—how nothing would have happened like in my dreams, or if it had, how horrible that would have been, and how maybe that stink coming from my mother, the liquor and the story of *her* mother and her tears in Kyle's studio, maybe that was her grief coming out. But then she went after Mark. Probably looking for more Interlochen money, when I'm not even going back. Or maybe just proving to herself and the world, like she always does, how beautiful she is.

The sun behind people on the boardwalk turns them into silhouettes. They walk alone or in pairs, cardboard cutouts, but mostly alone. With a dog maybe.

Like any kid I thought she'd find a guy she liked so much she'd marry him. I'd like him too, and we'd be a family, and they'd have other kids, my sisters and brothers. But she never did. And I don't know if there's something wrong with her because of that, if she thinks she's better than everyone, so full of herself, and just won't ever settle for less than best. But that's a lie because of Kyle. Because he was the best. Because there's no way she's finding someone better than him, which is what's so sick about her going after Cynthia's man.

I don't have to bury him today if I don't want to. I've been looking for a spot in the sand that seems right somehow, where the tide would wash over and take these feelings out to his ashes, but I don't have to do that today if I'm not ready to. Over the sound of the ocean I hear the whistle of the Long Island Rail Road, the cries of gulls and other birds, but mainly just the sound of the tide, the endless movement of water, which will always and forever remind me of Kyle.

Nikki

Even though I don't believe in dreams, I dream of that spot Downeast Maine where George and I camped all those years ago, when I was so young and had just run from Manchester and was finally free of my mother. I take an image of us on the beach at night into my dream, or us sitting on a log by the fire kissing or walking down by the water under the stars, that feeling of knowing everything was about to begin or had just begun, Alina in my memory or dream waiting to be born, because we didn't use birth control those few weeks we were together and I didn't care, didn't want to stop a baby from coming out of everything I felt for him.

We couldn't get enough of each other. I fell asleep touching him and woke reaching for him, and because we never had time to use each other up, I never have in my memory either—even though I hated him for leaving me on the street in Providence like he did. Even though I never heard from him or saw him again. But I never quite burned him out of my mind either, that week in Maine like the beginning of time, certainly the beginning of my life it felt like.

In Providence, I kept waiting for him to return with a good reason for having left, and then tried to cover that hole with hatred from the hurt. But even if something bad did happen to him, or if nothing happened, if something just went wrong and he disappeared, in my sleep or near sleep we can be at the beach together or in our tent, wanting a baby for the first and only time in my life, to create something beautiful out of all that love. And it's Alina of course, Alina, who, like him, I never grow tired of looking at or touching, those moments of fullness and potential and surrender stretching out with me in a dream forever. But he turns into Mark again and again, and I hate myself for this feeling in my guts, for having taken something there was no time to take, knowing I was only doing it for Alina. But losing myself like I did—allowing a kind of surrender I didn't have a right to and can't afford—feels unforgivable, a weight I can't stop dragging even in my dream.

MARK

I kept tasting Nikki's skin under beer and tequila, practically seeing her in my aunt's backyard. There was nothing I could do to help her if she was just going to run, and no way to come up with that kind of money so fast, but I kept tasting her skin, even as I felt the loss of Cynthia—not just her death, but everything we'd lost so many years before and never could have gotten back and never should have gone after again in the first place. I tried to forgive her for her involvement with Kyle, her love for Kyle, knowing it wasn't mine to forgive, sickened by this feeling of ownership and almost regretting trying to block her feelings for him, but whenever I thought of them dead together, I felt another stab of jealousy, and then I'd smell Nikki and taste her skin, afraid and exhilarated by the way she was infecting me, Cynthia saying, "What, so you hate me for loving Kyle? When you're already— whatever you are with this Nikki chick? At least what Kyle and I had was based on more than money."

"What about the baby?" I said.

"You don't know shit about the baby," Cynthia said. "You don't know shit about shit. Go help Nikki if you're so desperate to be a doormat."

There was nothing I could do to help Nikki though. I was sick of everything being finally and forever about money, which got me wrapped up wondering who would get hurt if Kara was paid again. What did I care if she got another bag of cash? I'd known she wanted to keep her baby that day at the lagoons, and I scared her out of it with threats I would have delivered on. Why shouldn't she get paid, over and over and over again?

I considered calling Liz to tell her I'd contact Kara, thinking only of Nikki really, how she was playing me for money I'd never be able to get and how I almost didn't care. But the way I kept tasting her skin on the patio and later, waking from sleep, made me afraid to help her—because I was so small—knowing part of me would expect something in return, everything, knowing that whatever was between us would amount to just another transaction, and how I wouldn't get enough out of the deal to make it worth my time or risk. I'd never be able to give her enough, either. The only thing to do was forget her and walk away, the only thing to do and exactly what I would do. But the taste of her skin, even in my sleep, the smell of her, awake, asleep, everywhere. . . .

BURKE

I get sort of lost in my imagined conversation with her, driving in traffic so early in the morning. "I really do understand," she says, touching my face. We're on lounge chairs pushed next to each other on the beach, the sound of waves washing up around us. "I'm just sorry for everything *you've* had to go through," she tells me, and I say, "I know you are, baby. I know everything about you."

We look at each other a second, her touching my face and sort of looking into my soul, and it's so intense, her studying me like that, all these minutes passing as we look at each other, and she finally says, "How come you love me so much, baby? Me just a whore," and I say, "Because you've got a pure heart is why. And a pure pussy and ass."

She laughs—"Naughty"—pressing her hand into my bathing suit.

"But, really, baby," I say. "Because you seem like a real human being is why."

"I love you, Daddy," she says, "I love you, Burke," because she knows my real name now, and I say, "I know you do. I love you too, Cinnamon."

But, then—that ain't even her real name. And I don't even want to know her real name. And I think, Fuck the hotel. Fuck the airport. Fuck sleep. And fuck that Cinnamon too, never telling me her real name, just a whore of Babylon like all the rest.

24

MARYELLEN

Children are a blessing and a curse, a blessing mostly, but the strength of the blessing making their power to hurt—you or themselves or the both of you—a curse maybe worse than the blessing. I never favored one child over the other, though both kinds, good and bad, will break your heart. I don't know what caused Burke to get into such trouble growing up, but I do know that a boy needs a man in his life. Billy Wayne was not much of a man for Burke, not much of model. At least, not the good kind.

Cash took after me, sweet and joyful and kind until they killed him over drugs down in Austin. I thought he was just getting his wildness out down there, that being close to the capital and the university might do him some good, just by being around those kinds of people. He was the smart one, the one with fire in his belly. I figured he'd go to college himself someday.

After Billy Wayne left, my mother took us in and helped raise the boys, but she also held them back, always telling me not to put ideas in their heads. I told them they could be whatever they wanted—an astronaut, a doctor, the president of the United States. Burke cared for Cash as much as I did during those thin gravy years, loved him and looked after him and was nearly as devastated as I was when they killed him. He tried so hard to make up for my

153

loss and be a good son, but there was nothing he could do to kill the pain and emptiness, no way for a man to understand that kind of loss even if he is from the same womb. You start to feel memory there only for the one they took, as if the lost one's the only one been inside you. Still, Burke and I became closer as result of my loss. I saw how hard he tried, working at that Denny's, out on the straight and narrow.

There was a girl Cash had at the end that he showed pictures of and told stories about, a Yankee girl from a broken home. You can read true love when you see it, and the way he talked about her, I knew that's just what he had. I was grateful that he got to taste a love like that. Given enough time, she probably would have saved him. They'd have saved each other, grown into their love and had children and moved away from the people in Austin trying to poison him, raised up a family and lived their lives in love, just like a fairy tale. That was the destiny I imagined in my dreams. My fairy tale, too.

Nobody knew Cash wasn't Billy Wayne's, that I'd also tasted true love. We only had one month together before they shipped him off to Vietnam, where he was probably killed, like so many of them were. Burke was two and Billy Wayne was gone most nights and I met a man stationed at Fort Hood, though we never had any contact after he left. Years later, when Cash talked about Nikki, I knew James and myself might have saved each other, too, given enough time and another set of circumstances. But I lost him before we got the chance.

All my memories and hurt over James came back when I lost Cash, became larger than they'd ever been, as if my love for him was growing through Cash's death, some kind of link through Cash to him on the other side. For a while it was as if I was no longer among the living myself, though I tried to hide my pain from Burke, tried to support him in his loss, too, because he'd always looked after his brother, always loved him, even if he did have a rough patch during his teen years and became what he became, nearly dragging Cash down with him. I knew Cash turned out well not just because of James's blood, but because of Burke being a father to him. That broke my heart to think, that Burke had sacrificed his childhood to father his brother. And for that brother—the one with all the real potential—to be snatched away just piled waste on top of waste.

I saw Burke change after Cash died, saw how hard he tried when he came home from Huntsville. Saw him turn into a better man than his daddy ever was. He'd never become Cash. He knew it and I knew it. Anyone would have known it. But he did become a better man. His love for me grew as mine grew for him, as mine grew for James, the result of all that loss. Even if he'd never amount to more than a short order cook, Burke did learn how to love, Cash's final gift from the other side.

Burke

Sometimes things work out better than you can even dream, one of the many surprising things about life and more proof of the guiding hand directing everything to a fateful purpose. I park the car and walk the boardwalk, then down to the beach and back to the boardwalk, where I sit on a bench smoking and drinking coffee and ruminating and flipping through pictures of Nikki and Cash and looking at the water, or off to the west, the towers of the city, the rat's nest so miniature and harmless from this distance, almost fake looking, the sky a perfect blue and cloudless, a train whistling behind me and the ocean crashing and people living their beach lives, which some of them might deserve to live, but which at least one of them don't, having murdered my brother in cold blood. I'm just easing through these morning hours, knowing I've got plenty of time to scope her house and break in and hide myself for her return from work, when I'll maybe tie her up like she tied Cash and cut off her clothes and lay down the death by a thousand cuts and watch *her* bleed like she bled Cash, but a lot slower, her begging for life, not at all like Cinnamon, but crying and begging and me resisting the temptation to give her back her miserable life, fighting that, or maybe deciding, based on what she says or does, to let her live, or to watch her bleed, depending, and then flying out of John F. Kennedy airport to San Diego or Puerto Rico, to settle on the beach with all that broad assed Puerto Rican cooze and all my money. But I know I got a hell of a lot more planning to do—because I have to get that pile of cash before any bleeding can happen, and I'm thinking after I smoke one more cigarette and finish my coffee, maybe I'll call her up, two days before I said I'd be in New York, to see if she's got the money together and to make plans for the exchange, to scare her into action and see if she's got the cops involved, maybe just to talk and then watch her house, to see if I can see when she picks up the money and brings it on home—the moment I'll go into phase two, tying her up and bleeding her—when I'll be goddamned if she herself don't walk through one of them netless volleyball pits down on the beach, carrying flip flops and heading toward the stairs up to the boardwalk not ten feet from the bench I'm sitting on. I rub my eyes and want to pinch myself to make sure this ain't a dream, she herself walking right toward me on what might now indeed be the day of reckoning, everything changing so fast, like she's ready for it too, surrendering to *her* destiny, my blood racing and not knowing if I should say anything or not, but her walking up the stairs looking right at me, like she's coming for *me* almost, then looking away, and I can't tell if she's scared or not, the sun behind her, but she don't seem scared, and as she turns to walk east on the boardwalk away from me I call her name.

ALINA

People mistake us on the phone sometimes and tell us we look alike, that we could be sisters, which my mother loves, but nobody ever thinks I *am* her, so when he calls her name I figure it must be because of the sun behind me. Even though I finally buried the wooden man on the beach, it still feels like I'm holding Kyle in the ball of my hands, and I don't feel like talking to anyone, especially some guy I don't know who's probably in love with her like all the rest. But then he says it again—"Hey, Nikki"—and when I turn, he looks kind of familiar and I see in his face that he's recognized his mistake, and I say, "Nope. Wrong number," and he says, "You must be. . . ."

And stands there looking at me.

NIKKI

I was awake all night and slept the morning away and now when I call her name, she doesn't answer. I run downstairs, telling myself she's on the porch or in the backyard, but she's nowhere. I call Ashley's mother, who hasn't seen her since last night. I call Long Beach High School, but Alina isn't there, wouldn't be allowed there, they tell me, until she's enrolled. I run to the beach, thinking she's lying in the sun or getting coffee or sitting on the boardwalk eating an ice, playing volleyball like she used to with Kyle.

But she's nowhere.

I call Mark and his phone rings and rings. If she's moving, she could be in all the spots I've already checked, walking ahead or behind me, but I can't just go home and wait. I walk, half running, up and down the boardwalk, then to Magnolia pier, where it's only fishermen, and I wonder if I should ask if anyone's seen her, but I don't know how long I've been gone or if I can even talk, and she's certainly home by now.

But the house is empty. And there's still no note.

I could have at least warned her that someone was out there, some sick fuck gunning for her. But I didn't because I was too sure of my power to protect her, certain I could keep her invisible, when she's so beautiful, when her walk and her hair and her smile and her eyes and everything about her screams look at me look at me look at me, and me so stupid, so goddamn stupid. Because he didn't know she existed I fooled myself into believing I could hide her and make her not exist—her, the only thing he could take from me, the only thing to protect. And he got her, all that sickness, all that disease in his blood. I call Mark again and he answers and I ask him to come right now, everything boiling in my stomach and throat, nearly choking me, so I can hardly talk, and I say, "Please," and he says, "What's going on?" and I say, "Please."

Mark

Nikki was on the sidewalk when I pulled in front of her house, something frantic in her eyes and the rigid hold she had on her body, her forehead smeared with ink or ash.

"Come on," she said, approaching me as I got out of the car. "I have to tell you—"

She looked at me for a second, a deep fatigue in her eyes and all over her face. "Here," she said. "We'll sit on the porch." She put her hand to the smeared spot on her forehead. "He might drive by," she said. "We should go inside."

She opened the door and I followed her into the kitchen.

"We don't have time," she said, looking into a cabinet over the sink, her back to me. Frozen. But with a tremor running through her.

"What is it?" I said.

She turned around, a blank intensity in her eyes.

I waited for her to say what she had to say.

She ran her hand over her forehead.

"Talk to me," I said. "Tell me."

"Just," she said. "I don't—"

And once she started, she couldn't stop, laying herself open, everything she hadn't said the night before, a rape, this prick Burke coming after her from prison, her daughter already missing. I held onto her, standing in her kitchen, then went with her to the floor as she talked as fast as she could, a river of words pouring out of her, her fear working itself into my guts as if I'd swallowed a broken piece of it.

25

ALINA

"Alina Fiore," I say. "Who are you?"

"Steve," he says, walking toward me and offering his hand. "LeRoy."

I take his hand and let it go. "Nice to meet you, Steve LeRoy."

I turn to walk away, and he says, "I knew your mama, Alina—way back when—in Texas," and I stop cold, because of whatever it was I recognized in his face or ears or eyes, whatever it was that made me know without knowing, what I've been waiting for all these years, all my life. But it can't be true, even if I do feel a shiver of knowing, because there's no way for it to be true.

"You must've been born after she left," he says. "Come on. I'll show you some pictures from way back when. Of your mama."

He beckons me toward the bench he's been sitting on, looking out toward the ocean, and I feel myself pulled to the pictures he waves in his hand. "Come on and sit," he says, patting the bench. "Your mama and me was close down in Austin," and I think it can't be true, even though I know it is.

Maybe I don't want to know. Maybe I'm not ready.

"Look at this," he says, handing me a picture of him and her standing on a rock in a nearly dried up river. "She wasn't much older than you are now."

I look from the old picture of my mom and him up to the real version of him now—my father finally right in front of me—then back to the picture of him and my mother so happy before I was born, or maybe she was even pregnant with me then—I know she got pregnant in Austin—her and my father on a rock in a river in Texas, and now he's right here with me, part of me hating him for waiting all these years and part of me wanting to know everything about him. I remember how often she told me he never even knew I existed, and I say, "Did you know about me?"

He looks at me for a long minute, sort of studying me, and finally says, "No, I didn't, Alina," and I say, "But how did you find out?"

He hands me a picture of him and my mother on the porch of some farmhouse they maybe lived in together. "Didn't she tell you about me?"

"Here's another," he says, then snatches it back and says, "Ooops. That one's kind of—what's the word? Inappropriate."

I reach for it, sort of desperate to look at the stupid thing.

"Not to me it ain't," he says. "But you know how people are."

"Let me see it," I say, not knowing if I want to see it. Not knowing if I want to know this man at all, knowing, of course, that I want to know everything about him, but afraid too, and pissed that he could just appear like this. But also knowing it's not his fault, because she never told him about me, hating her for how she treats me like some object she possesses or something else to control in her life, always trying to decide what's good for me or bad without really knowing at all, and how she treated Kyle, and how she thinks she's better than everyone, and how my father didn't die like she said he did in some accident, which I knew all along—just because of how his name would change.

"Come on," I say, reaching for the picture. "I can handle it."

"You can, huh?" he says, holding the picture close to himself. "How old are you, Alina?"

"Thirteen," I tell him, kind of angry he doesn't know, that he can't do the math, but maybe my mother was just—nothing to him. Except that he's here now and has these pictures of the two of them down in Texas.

"You know what?" he says. "I think you've got as much right as anyone to look at a picture of your own mama," and he hands me the photo, my mother on a bed topless, leaning against a headboard and smiling, practically my age, and there's nothing dirty about it, she's not trying to be sexy, she just doesn't have a shirt on, and she's never been modest in any way—I've seen her nude thousands of times. She's just so young and beautiful and her smile so huge, lighting her up, and just like in the river picture I look for evidence of myself in her body, tiny inside her. I see him in my mind behind the camera taking the picture, the man she's smiling at, both of them there, my mother and father, all this evidence that they existed together and were happy, and me between them, invisible, already alive and just waiting to be born.

Nikki

Mark doesn't understand why I can't go to the cops, even after I tell him about Cash bleeding out on the couch at Duval. "But that was self-defense," he says. "From back at your apartment," and I tell him again how I have no way to prove that, how I didn't do anything to stop the bleeding, how my cousin disappeared off the face of the earth, is probably dead herself by now—I would have heard from her otherwise, long ago—how Alina and I have no family but each other, how I killed Cash—I killed him—and he says, "But nobody knows that, and nobody came after you."

"Burke knows it!"

"He doesn't know it. He's guessing. And what you did was self-defense."

"He does know it, and he already told me." I see Burke and Alina again, Burke maybe touching her this very second—which I can't—or driving her dead in the trunk of his car, her body broken, and I let go again, feeling like I'm going to throw up, and he's holding me, saying, "It's going to be okay. What do you want me to do first?"

"The money," I say. "In case he calls."

"But that's why we should go to the cops," he says.

"No!" I say. "He'll kill her," and I tell him again what he told me on the phone weeks ago, what he'd do to me if I went to the cops, which never scared me, except I'd never abandon her, but now it's much worse, because now he'll do it to her. But maybe he doesn't even have her, because maybe he doesn't—it's possible—maybe she just walked and walked, all the way to Point Lookout and back, to Montauk and back, walking, Burke not even in New York at all, having no idea in the world of her, her just walking all these hours since I woke and she was gone. And even though I hate myself for my hope, I say, "I'm going back out. You stay here—in case they come back. But don't let them see you. And don't scare her if she comes alone."

"I won't scare her," he says.

Somehow I've landed back in his embrace. I'm holding on to him.

"And the money," I say, "the money," and he says, "I'll get it. Go."

BURKE

I know everything by the way Alina looks at me once I show her the pictures, all this raw hunger in her face. She thinks I'm her daddy—thinks I'm Cash—and I let her think it, sort of bringing him to life through my impersonation. And once I figure it out, which must be the same second she figures it out, which is pretty much immediately—the guiding hand of fate bringing us together—Cash starts coming out in her more, making himself visible in her attached earlobes or the ways she tilts her head, sort of sly like Cash was and playful, except she's got all this confusion and hurt running over her face.

"Did you know when you saw me?" I ask her. "When you heard my name?"

"She lied," Alina says, pinching her eyebrows like Cash.

"Don't blame her now," I say.

"Said your name was Jim. Or Dan."

"Try not to be hurtful," I tell her.

"She said you died!"

"Well, now—"

"But I knew it wasn't true, because of how your name would change. And how she wouldn't talk about you no matter how much I begged."

"That's the trauma of true love, Alina. It can work in mysterious ways. Especially when you're so young."

"And also because—I just *knew* you were alive. Because of this feeling I had. But sometimes I didn't know. Sometimes I believed her."

"Well, I'm here, now, that's for sure. And we got all kinds of time to catch up."

I hand her a picture of Nikki and me out on 6th street in Austin.

It's so typical of that bitch not to tell Alina one goddamn thing about her daddy, what every child has a right to know. She'll have to pay for the rest of her life now. No reason whatsoever to slaughter that milk cow. I'll take her out later, torture her and take her out later, everything she's done, everything she's taken, which I only knew part of before. But now I know she's been running up debt with interest all these years gone by, and

164

it'll be like how the courts do, garnishing a man's wages to pay for the babies his bitch wife's stolen, even if she is a cheating whore or crank addict, humping everything in pants. No matter any of that, he's still got to pay. But not this time. Because this time it's her that's got to pay.

We flip through the pictures, one by one, and I tell her that's the Colorado River in that picture, and that's a house we lived in on Duval Street, and how we met at a concert back of Stubb's and fell in love from the moment we laid eyes on each other, her wearing that leather skirt like in the picture of the two of us at Stubb's counter, and me wearing that stupid cowboy hat from the picture of us down by the river, and how we were inseparable from the moment we laid eyes on each other.

She's got emotion all over her face when she looks at me—love and whatnot—and I say, "Come here, baby," and take her in my arms like she is my daughter, which she practically is, the same blood running through us, and she cries against me, wrapping her arms around my neck and squeezing as she sniffles, while I map out the story that will keep her close and believing until I can call Nikki and tell her what I got, all these people walking behind us on the boardwalk or down on the beach, and she says, "But how did you find me," and she sits up looking at me, "if you didn't know?"

I reach out to run a piece of hair behind her ear. She is my blood. That's the thing of it. Even if I am working her for money, she is my blood. Practically my own daughter, with Cash dead and gone.

"We fought over you," I tell her.

"But I thought you didn't know."

"I knew and I didn't know," I tell her. "Just like you. You knew and you didn't know. That's the guiding hand of fate, then doubt working against it. I knew your mama was pregnant. That's what we fought over—what your mama wanted to do."

Her face maps the wheels turning in her head as she tries to put it together, but I'm miles ahead of her.

"Your mama was young," I tell her. "I don't want you to blame her now. She was very young. Both of us was. Maybe the reason our love was so pure."

"So she wanted—"

"She didn't know what she wanted. You know how bullheaded she can be. She wouldn't admit to being confused. Thought she wasn't ready for a baby, what she said anyways. But I wouldn't let her do it. That's what we fought over."

It breaks my heart to think of all the years I missed watching her grow up, everything Cash missed and keeps missing, this sweet little girl almost a woman who Nikki ain't even poisoned against him. It's much worse than that. She's erased him, killed him and then erased him from his baby's life. More of a monster than I ever dreamed possible.

"She never told me that," she says staring out at the ocean.

"Sounds like she didn't tell you much."

"She didn't tell me anything."

I run my hand in circles over her back as she stares at the water and then looks at me with Cash's eyes.

"I want to tell you how in love we were," I say, "and just exactly what happened between us. You got to be somewhere?"

I run that hair behind her ear again as she looks at the water sniffling.

"I don't have to be anywhere," she says.

"Let's get some pie then," I tell her. "And talk. Just you and me. You like pie?"

"I like pie," she says, and I say, "Me, too," and we walk the boardwalk, a father and daughter reunited after all these years apart and so much to learn about one another. I'm thinking she'll have to pay the fifty thousand for starters, then pay once a year, maybe twenty grand or thirty, depending on what she earns.

But I'll have to keep her close to make sure she don't slip away again.

There's other families around us, mothers and babies or mothers and toddlers, the little ones that ain't in school. I'll want to see Alina at least once a week to watch her last years growing up, and to make sure Nikki don't try to snatch her again and run. Although I found her once, the second I started trying, so if I do end up in Puerto Rico, traveling from one beach to the next, I can always find her again. Because of the blood—because of blood finding blood like a magnet to iron.

26

Nikki

I walk through the heat of another hundred degree day, half running and scanning the beach and boardwalk, trying to find places he could have left her body, trying to make myself as strong as I've always been, focused on finding her and the forward movement of my legs. I scramble into the low dunes crisscrossed with rickety erosion fences, thinking she might be leaning against one of those, or maybe lying in one of the depressions, but she's not, and I haven't checked the coffee shops or restaurants where she could be reading or eating lunch, because she could be anywhere, and in my head begging—please, please, please—not even noticing it most of the time, just, please, please, please—trying to believe in god and not believing, because I've never believed, never once even considered believing in something that's so much about trying to believe in itself, something that's always felt like a magic trick, a hidden door finally opening to nothing when you completely surrender to the delusion.

But trying to believe anyway, promising anything. I'll do anything. Remembering how her hair grew in dark like mine after her reddish baby hair fell out, thinking that mark on her of Cash would be gone forever, remembering the relief I felt after dropping her at Interlochen—as though I'd gotten away with something—and not needing to make any promises then, because I would deal with Burke alone and Alina would stay safe in Michigan and there would be no way for him to find out about her, but promising now anything—I'll do anything if you give her back to me. Anything. I will do anything.

But not knowing what to exchange. Anything. And then I think, I'll take him and You can take me. But just make sure Alina's okay. Give her to Mark to raise and protect and take care of and love—I'll believe he can do that, if You make it true. I'll believe if You make it true, and I'll take him and You can take me and then give her to Mark and he'll love her because I'll believe now and forever. And believing will make it true.

ALINA

We walk through town and into the Long Beach Diner, where we order pie and coffee and then lunch, my father telling me about himself and about them together. He's so different than I thought he would be as he turns into himself, so different than I ever imagined, so handsome and sweet and funny, but also sort of rough, the way he talks and the tattoos on his arms, which he shows me when I ask, telling me the story of each one and finally even telling me he went to prison for drugs, looking at me hard and putting his hand under my chin, saying, "I want you to promise me here and now, Alina, that you won't ever take drugs—even if you are out of your mind with grief and lovesickness, like I was when your mama ran away with you in her belly."

I nod and he says, "Say it," and I say it, because I'll say anything and it will be true.

And then his chicken fried steak comes, which I've never known anyone to order. He has me taste it and tells me how much I'd have loved my granny's chicken fried steak—that's the word he uses, "Granny," my granny—and how there are so many things I have to know, like about my great granddaddy dying in World War II before he got a chance to see his baby daughter, or about my granny Priscilla, what a sweet old lady, and how my dad's own daddy left him when he was just four years old, so he never knew him, just like I haven't known *him,* but how that ain't the way it's going to be from now on, because everything's going to be different now that he's found me, him and me making up for lost time and being part of each other's lives from here on out forever.

I ask a bunch of questions and look at him a lot and listen, and he looks at me a lot and listens, and he's such a good storyteller, giving me a past I never knew I had, so that my whole life, my whole self, seems to become so much larger. He tells me how he found me, how tortured he was by my mother leaving like she did—which I know a hundred percent is true, because she always leaves everyone and everything—her running from him and his desperate search for her, still so in love. He knew in his heart she still loved him too, because you do know that kind of thing, his desperate search for her dragging him into drugs and hating himself and just wanting to be dead, because he felt so empty and incomplete without her. But before all that was their last awful fight, the fight that made her run and lasted for days, when she finally told him she was just going to go on and do it, get rid of me, whether he liked it or not, because it was none of his damn business, my own father, *none of his damn business,* even though he told her he'd take me and raise me himself if she wanted nothing to do with me.

He tried so hard to convince her, begging her to wait just one more day. He thought if he could stretch it out hour by hour and day by day and week by week she'd surely come to love me as much as he already did—because he could feel me in his heart or soul, even if he couldn't feel me in his body like maybe she could. But she was just so confused and bullheaded, so set against having me, maybe because of how they were fighting so hard over what she was going to do to me.

That's what he regretted most, how he fought her and fought her, and how maybe their love got buried in those fights just a little, even though it was still there as strong as ever, but maybe it got hidden a little under so many harsh words about me and my fate, the guiding hand of fate always so mysterious, just another way to talk about the mystery of God or existence or whatever you like, and how he feared that their last fight— the last time they spoke, harsh words lingering over all that was left of them—how he feared those harsh words might have actually pushed her toward doing what he thought she'd done, and how it was all his fault, all of it, tears running down his face in the diner he doesn't even notice as he tells me it was all his fault.

"No!" I say, reaching out to him and crying myself. "No it wasn't!"

He takes my hand and we lace our fingers, crying and looking as each other and smiling too. "You tried," I tell him. "It was her! But then she didn't even do it." And I know how lucky I am to be alive. "Maybe because of all the things you said."

"And because of the love between us," he says. "Because you were—because you are—a symbol of that eternal love."

The waitress pours us more coffee without even asking, both of us crying and smiling and laughing, because of how close we've become so fast, which feels so perfectly natural. So *right*.

"But I have to beg your forgiveness, Alina," he says. "With all my heart," and I squeeze his fingers and say, "No, you don't!" and he says, "Please listen, sugar; then you can decide," and he tells me how he thought—after she disappeared and left him

171

so broken and heartsick and wanting to die and falling into drugs—that she actually *had* done it, because of how he couldn't feel me anymore—I was completely gone from him—and how he even thought he knew the moment she done it, this tearing inside, and how I was gone from him then for years, buried under the fog of drugs, but how in prison he became haunted by me, having dreams of me, which he suddenly knew he'd been having all along, also buried under the fog of drugs. He understood then that he'd been trying to bury me all along, to deny my existence, which he hated himself for more and more as the feeling of me became more vivid in his dreams—"And I know that might sound foolish," he says, "some kind of hippy dippy bullcrap, which is why I didn't tell no one about it, even as the dreams and feelings became stronger as the years wore on and I came to know for a certainty that you were out in the world alive, and so angry with myself for turning my back on you like I did."

"It's okay," I say. "Because I did that, too. Because I knew you were alive, but sometimes believed her—that you were dead."

That's when I know that part of her is probably still in love with him, which is probably why she didn't love Kyle enough, because she was still so in love with my real dad, even if her pride keeps her from admitting that he was right all along and she was wrong, even if she can't admit to her love, hiding her feelings for him under her pride, all of it explaining so much about her.

"Does my mom know," I ask him, "that you know about me now?"

"I couldn't risk it," he says.

"But maybe—"

"No, Alina," he says. "Let's not go too fast. I couldn't bear to lose you again."

"I'm not going anywhere," I tell him, and he smiles his big

bright smile at me, and says, "Neither am I, baby. Never again."

I am completely full with him, the guiding hand of fate uniting us, my *father*.

27

MARK

I called Liz again, got her voicemail again, and felt the old rush running through me, like I was finally waking—groggy but clearing—from a two-year nap. I made a pot of coffee and sat at Nikki's table, then walked from room to room. Upstairs in the hallway I looked at a nude of Nikki, something disturbing in it I couldn't figure out, until I realized Kyle had painted it, and then, weirder and worse, that he'd given her Cynthia's eyes— blazing from Nikki's face, attached to Nikki's body. I heard a car pull to the curb and ran down to the kitchen to hide, thinking I could creep out the back door if the front door opened. But there was nothing.

I called Liz again, got her voicemail again. I'd give her what she wanted and she'd set me up with money for Nikki. And if she couldn't do it—but she would do it. I'd give her what she wanted, and she'd get me what I needed. I knew Nikki should go to the cops, had tried to convince her, but she wouldn't hear it. She thought her only chance of keeping Alina safe was not going to the cops. I almost called them myself, thought maybe I still would. I heard the screen door open and ducked into the kitchen, but it was Nikki, looking worse than when she'd left an hour ago, washed out and dead in her eyes. She rummaged through a kitchen drawer. "You have to start looking," she said.

She handed me a school picture of Alina. "She could be any-where," she said. "You have to keep your eyes open."

I took the picture.

"What about the money?" she said, and I said, "I'm working on it," and she said, "You don't have it?" and I said, "I'm waiting for a call."

"It probably doesn't even matter," Nikki said.

I tried to sit her at the table, but she couldn't stay still. She stood in kitchen, running her hands up and down her arms like she wanted to rub the skin off.

"It's okay," I said. "It's gonna be okay."

"Listen," she said. "If something happens to me."

"Nothing's going to happen to you."

"But if something does."

The telephone rang.

She looked at me and then at the phone on the wall.

"Answer it," I said.

She touched the phone and it rang again and she jerked her hand away.

"Go ahead, Nikki," I said.

Her hands were shaking.

"Come on now," I said. "Pick it up."

She took a step back.

I lifted the phone from the cradle and handed it to her.

BURKE

I call from a payphone in a little hall back by the bathrooms, Alina sitting in the dining room composing herself after all the tears we've shed. I don't know how much longer I can keep her from home, and while that might not matter much in the long run, it seems best if I get the money before Nikki starts lying to her about who I really am. I half wish I could hold onto her forever and never undo what I've told her, most of which is exactly true, everything about her granny and great granny and everyone else up the line, stories about growing up in Waco, and practically being her father anyway, taking on that guiding responsibility Nikki tried so hard to destroy when she murdered Cash. But knowing, as part of that responsibility, that I have to get the money first and foremost. Even the stories about Nikki and Cash probably 97 percent true, given all his crazy lovesickness and the way she treated him and her name tattooed on his arm.

She answers on the third ring and I say, "Hey, Nikki," and she says, "Where are you?" in this broken voice, and I say, "It don't matter where I am. Do you have the money?"

"I'm working on it," she says. "Where are you?" and I say, "That's not very encouraging—*working* on it," and she says, "No, I am," and I say, "How much?" and she says, "All of it. Where are you?"

She's breathing hard through the phone, scared.

"Why'd you kill my brother?" I say, "when he loved you so much."

"I didn't kill your brother," she says.

"Yes, you did."

"Where are you?"

"Where are *you*?"

"I'm working on getting the money."

"You're a killer," I say. "And a liar. A whore."

"I'm working on it right now," she says.

"Why'd you want to kill my brother's baby?"

An old lady pushes through the dining room's swinging door and back into the little hallway, smiling at me. I smile back and press myself against the wall so she can get to the restroom, Nikki saying, "I don't know what you're talking about. Cash and me—I never hurt your brother."

I cup my hand around the phone's mouthpiece up against

176

my face and whisper: "Is that what you told Alina all these years gone by?"

It's a perfect moment where everything changes just like I thought it would, all the air sucking out of Nikki's lungs as she finally recognizes the guiding hand of fate she thought all these years to avoid.

She gets her breath back as I wait, fast shallow things, and says, "Where is she?"

"Safe with me," I say.

"Where are you?"

"Did you love my brother as much as he loved you?"

"Yes," she says. "Where's Alina?"

"Safe with her daddy," I say.

"With her—no. No, she's not."

Her trying to breathe.

"What did you—"

Her suffocating.

"Who she thinks is her daddy," I say. "She thinks I'm him."

"Is she—"

"She's finally got a daddy," I say. "Killing him wasn't enough, was it Nikki? You had to take from him even after that, killing him every single day, never letting his baby know his name. Never giving his baby a name to remember him by."

"I'm getting the money," she says. "Just—where is she?"

The sound of her strangling. These fast, shallow, hiccup breaths.

"Where—"

"Maybe I'll keep her," I say. "How would that be? Teach her who she is. Where she comes from."

"No," she says. "I can't—"

"Shut up, Nikki," I say. "Just shut the fuck up."

She moans, the sound of angels celebrating this deliverance of justice, the sound of redemption and righteousness and my brother's liberation, after all these years suffering.

"What do you—"

"I said shut up, Nikki, and I mean it. I'll wait all day, if that's what you want."

"No, I'm just—"

"There it is again. I say shut up and you keep talking. As if you don't care a thing about her."

She struggles to breathe the poison all around her, taking sips and practically squeaking, and I wonder if I can kill her like this, just by making her try to quiet herself as she struggles to breathe the air she's poisoned with her lies and killing and smearing of my brother and our name.

"That's right, Nikki," I say. "Take a nice deep breath. That's right. And again."

The bathroom door opens, and I say into the phone, "Just a minute, baby," and make myself small by the wall so the old lady can get past me, her smiling and me smiling right back. And then she's gone, back in the dining room, the door swinging behind her.

"Don't say a word now, Nikki. Not one fucking word," and I tell her about the guiding hand of fate you can't ever escape, how destiny makes blood hungry to find itself, and what a goddamn fool she's been all these years to think she escaped the guiding hand that would come back and punish her for murdering my brother in cold blood, and then making everything so much worse—what a goddamn fool she is—by denying him to his child, denying his child to him, denying the blood, like trying to stop a river's floodwaters with piles of sand, but the sand turned to poison now, infecting everything as it fans out with the water. Taking my time to listen to her ragged, killing breaths.

"Do you understand what I'm saying, Nikki?"

Just those raggedy breaths.

"You can talk now."

"What do you want?" she says.

178

"I asked you a question."

The squeaking sound.

"Do. You. Under. Stand?"

"I—"

"About. The guiding. Hand?"

"Yes," she says.

"Alina thinks you're in love with him," I say. "With me. Is that true?"

"Yes," she says. "I never stopped loving him."

"Don't lie to me, Nikki. I hate a liar like I hate a killer. Like I hate a whore."

"It is true," she says. "I never stopped loving him."

"Say it now. What I called you."

"I don't—"

"You're a killer," I say. "Say that. And a liar. A whore."

"I'm a killer," she says. "And a liar. And a whore."

The door swings open from the dining room, and there's Alina herself, sort of putting her hand to her mouth in surprise at interrupting me on the phone in this narrow hallway, then pointing to the bathroom behind me.

I hold up a finger, smiling with my whole face, and it's a whole true smile, her so beautiful and kind and sweet and deprived all these years. The door swings shut behind her and she stands looking at me, glowing.

"I wish you'd go on and tell her that, Nikki," I say into the phone. "We've been here catching up. I didn't know how best to go about it, but I couldn't wait no more."

"Where—"

"I know it's been an awful surprise," I say, "but I just had to. . . ," and I sort of choke up for a second looking at Alina looking at me and reaching for the phone. I hold up my finger again. "She just looks so much like you," I say, "taking me deep into all our time together, all our love, all I thought we'd lost. . . ."

I nod at Alina with my finger still in the air.

"Me too," I say. "Just a second."

I palm the phone's mouthpiece.

"Go on to the bathroom," I tell Alina. "She just wants to talk a minute more to me. We got so much catching up to do. Then she wants to talk to you."

Alina beams as she makes her way into the bathroom.

I whisper into the phone. "I want that money now, Nikki. Today."

"Please," Nikki says. "Just let me talk to her."

"Listen," I say. "Tell her I'm her father, and nothing more. And don't act all crazy. Tell her, 'Steve's your daddy.'"

"Steve?"

"Get it together," I whisper. "Say 'I want you to spend some time with Steve. With your daddy.' Say that right now so I can hear it."

She says it like a robot.

And I know it ain't gonna work.

"Listen," I whisper. "That ain't no good. You have that money ready when I call back. And don't even think about the cops. I got somebody watching you, Nikki, who you ain't never gonna know is there, hidden on Wyoming Avenue. So if there's any sign at all of the cops, you can just say goodbye—"

The bathroom door swings open behind me. "Okay, baby," I say into the phone. "I'll tell her. Yes. I will. I love you, too," and I hang up, Alina there waiting.

"She's too broken up," I tell her. "Wants us to call back in a little while."

"Let's just go over there," Alina says. "We can sit on the porch or in the backyard. We can walk down to the beach."

"We will, baby," I say. "All that and more. That's just what she wants to do. But we'll call her back first. In a bit. She just wants a little time to get used to the idea is all, to get herself together. There's a lot of emotion running through her. Exactly like you said. What I never dared hope. All that love of ours like a rising river inside her."

I usher her out the hallway and back to the dining room, not sure of my next move. But knowing we have to keep moving.

"Is that okay?" I ask her. "If you and me spend a little more time together before going back home?"

She nods as fast and shallow as Nikki's breaths on the phone, and I can see how hard she's trying to keep from crying as I radiate my love toward her, all my love radiating, and my future out on the beach waiting.

28

NIKKI

29

GAIL

We'd fly out over the country or up into space, just the two of us, before Nikki was born, or holding her as a swaddled baby—just the three of us, like astronauts above the big beautiful earth, all blue and dreaming down below. I gave her Michael's name, hoping he'd come back and claim her. Fiore. My beautiful little flower. That's what she was for so long—my beautiful little flower. We'd fly up over the planet in our body ships, Michael and me, no sign on him of the agent orange poison that killed him, sometimes with Nikki and sometimes without, but always together, searching for Alina, born or unborn, entwined, our bodies whole and young and beautiful as we flew into eternity.

MARK

I watched the emotions play across her face, a deep relief finally sending her to the floor. "No," she said into the phone. "Wait," she said, after he hung up. "Wait!"

I went to the floor with her, but didn't touch her. She seemed to be holding herself tight. I reached out and put a hand on her shoulder and she fell into me.

"You think you'd be able to tell," she said. "But I can't. He said she was—I mean—but why should I believe him? Part of me thinks she was, because—for just a minute—I could almost see her. He wanted me to say, 'Steve's your daddy.' That's what he called himself. Steve. And I'm like—but then he's like."

"It's going to be okay," I said.

"Her daddy," Nikki said. "I can't—"

She put her hand to her mouth, her eyes closed tight.

"I think she was there," she said. "Just how his tone changed. Like he was acting. I think that might be a good thing."

"It's definitely a good thing," I said. "But he's going to call again. And that's why we should call the cops."

"No!" she said. "He said someone was watching the house— here on Wyoming Avenue. He said I wouldn't see them, but they're watching, and he'll kill her the minute he knows something's wrong—if he even suspects something's wrong. I know he might be lying, but I can't take that kind of risk."

"Of course not," I said, my mind racing, knowing I probably had no shot at the money with so little time, thinking my only chance was maybe—but it was ridiculous. "So, when do we need the money?" I said.

"Soon," she said. "You have to get it now."

"I'll get it," I said, knowing I wouldn't be able to get it. Knowing I'd have to do it the other way. "I'll sneak out the back door," I said.

"But what if someone sees you?"

"They won't," I said. "I'll sneak out and get the money and bring it right back."

She walked me through the kitchen.

"But you can't let them see you."

"No one will see me."

"You'll bring the money back and leave again," she said, "because I have to be alone here," and I said, "Sure, I will. Of course, I will," knowing I wouldn't let her face that shithead by herself.

NIKKI

When the phone rang again, I couldn't dare hope she was okay, but I couldn't talk to him without knowing.

"Five o'clock, Nikki," he said, "and we're watching you."

The sound of his voice like Cash and so much worse.

"Do you have it?"

"I'm getting it," I said, thinking of Mark, but also the money I'd already gathered, sitting at the bank. "But I have to talk to her."

"No, Nikki," he said. "You'll talk to her when I say you can talk to her."

"I have to talk to her now," I said. "And I have to leave the house to pick up the money."

"You can leave the house," he said, "but if you go to the cops or if you call the cops or if someone else calls the cops or if a cop drives by on your street or if someone who looks like a cop drives by on your street—she's dead, Nikki. And you ain't never gonna see her again."

"I have to talk to her," I said, and it was like I was in this tunnel, everything black around a tiny circle of light I was staring at five hundred miles away.

"No," he said.

And I knew again what he'd done to her and I told him again that I had to hear her voice to know she was okay.

"You'll hear her after I get paid," he said, and I said, "I can't wait that long," and he said, "You'd rather she was dead? Is that what you're saying to me?" and I said, "I'm not saying that— please—but imagine not knowing and not being able to do anything until you know. Not being able to breathe even. I want to do what you want me to do, but I'm saying I have to know—I'm saying I can't get my breath. I have to know like you would have to know—"

"Shut the fuck up, Nikki. I'm the one saying what happens, here."

"I know," I said, hoping as hard as I could and trying to breathe. "Except for this one thing. Because I have to. Just as you would have to. Because of your love. Just exactly what you would have to—"

"You goddamn!" And then the phone smacking against something, and knowing again what he'd done to her, letting out this moan, like he'd kicked me in the stomach and was still kicking me, knowing I'd never see her again or touch her, but saying, "Are you there?" and nothing, and, "Are you there?" and nothing, and, "ARE YOU THERE? and him finally saying, "You goddamn—you filthy—but if you say anything—if you—we're going to goddamn," and I thought, Okay, and I said, "Okay, just let me—"

"And remember," he said, "I'm her father. Steve. You goddamn." And he told me a few other things, but I couldn't listen and couldn't see and couldn't breathe because she was so close, and it wasn't until I heard her voice that I would breathe, and then it was waves of euphoria, even as I held myself back, the beautiful sound of her voice, even knowing he was listening and that if I gave anything away he'd do everything I'd already imagined. But not yet, because she was fine in the moment. Upset, but with me, because of all the lies he'd told her, which she told me now, that he was her father denied by me, and also that she was so happy to finally be with him, to meet him, to spend time with him. I just had to flatten myself, waves of revulsion following waves of euphoria, not letting her know the danger she was in, no way of telling her without increasing the danger, so flattening myself and not letting her know anything, and knowing in the moments inside the sound of her voice that she was alive and unharmed, which was plenty, more than enough, everything, as long as I could hear her, but even in the moments of knowing she was alive, I dreaded hanging up and having to wait again, and no idea where he had her or what he'd do, but he hadn't done anything yet and that would be enough until I could see her, and her saying, "But we want to come now," him in the background saying her name, and I remembered what he told me—that they wouldn't come until five, when I had the money, and her saying, "Why can't we just," and him saying her name, and me finally saying, "No, baby. In just a little while. I want to make everything nice. I want to make everything ready," and her spewing this awful poison from him. But it's nothing. As long as I can hear the sound of her voice.

And then she hangs up.

He hasn't hurt her yet. He might. But he hasn't hurt her.

And if he does—

I bring my toolbox up from the basement. Take out the hammer. Two big Phillips head screwdrivers and a standard screwdriver. Just in case. An exacto blade. Could I have said something that would have made her know, that would have alerted her to the danger? Run? That man is a liar? A killer? Even minutes off the phone, I can't think of a coded way I could have told her. I can hardly think of anything. I jam the big kitchen knife, blade down, into the planter on the landing near the bottom of the stairs, hiding its handle under drooping leaves. I put my hammer by the toaster on the kitchen counter, a screwdriver beside the TV, a screwdriver between couch cushions, a screwdriver under a newspaper on the kitchen table. There was nothing I could have said to warn her. Not without risking everything. And now it will just be a matter of giving him money and him leaving and then me telling her everything that led to this, none of which matters anymore. A boning knife on the toilet tank under a magazine. Two steak knives under each pillow on my bed. Just in case. Trying to grab for the euphoria at the sound of her voice fading, alternating waves of euphoria and revulsion, a box cutter on the mantle under some dried flowers, and still hours to go.

I take Cash's finger bone from its pink, silk pouch and scrape it across my palm, creating a weird itch in my open hand as I rub the chip across it, waiting and waiting, because if not the knife or the hammer, maybe the bone. Just to prove. To show how much. The fact that I still have it. Just to prove.

ALINA

He's got a rental car and wants me to show him around and tell stories about myself connected to places, but I don't really know how to get anywhere once we're up on the main island out of Long Beach. I ask if we can maybe go home now, because I want us to all be together, not even afraid that she'll act the way she always does because of how I heard him talking to her on the phone back at the diner.

He pulls into a gas station with an old phone booth on the corner and sends me inside with a twenty dollar bill to get some soda and candy and other "provisions" I might think we need. "I just want to talk to your mama alone a minute," he says, "to see if she's ready for us."

"She will be," I say, because how could she not love him?

But apparently not.

Because when I get on the phone, she sounds half dead. Bored. Exactly the opposite of how I thought she'd be—which was finally accepting of all these things I deserve to know, finally believing I can take care of myself, which I'm not even by myself, but with my own father! For the first time in my life! But she's all distracted, like with Kyle, like she can't ever care about anything but herself and whatever it is she's thinking about herself, how beautiful she is probably, and how everyone falls in love with her, even if she is completely selfish. She says we can't come home yet because she wants to take a bath first. That she's cleaning. *That she's cleaning*! That we can come at five, but to call first.

All this after I told her how excited I was! How happy!

She doesn't care about any of that. At all.

"Why did you keep him from me?" I ask her, him in the phone booth with me, shaking his head.

"Give her space," he whispers. "Give her time."

He doesn't know her like I do.

She says, "Let's talk about this later, Alina. We'll have dinner together."

"Let's talk about it now," I say.

Steve—my dad—keeps shaking his head, reaching for the phone in my hand. "Let it go now," he says. "Give her space."

"He doesn't deserve to be treated that way!" I tell her. "Neither do I."

And I hang up on her.

Steve—my dad—understands that I need some time to be angry, and we end up driving past Jones Beach, mostly quiet in the car together, and then out the Ocean Parkway all the way to Robert Moses, where he drives in the traffic circle around the big tower six or seven times, looking at me and grinning until I have to laugh with him as we go round and round, because he's so funny and sensitive and acts exactly like a father should. And even though that makes me kind of sad, or mad again, I decide to just let it go. I ask him to park so we can walk the beach together, where I push her away from myself, from us, for just a little longer, just a little while, until the three of us can finally be together for good.

30

MARK

I snuck through a neighbor's yard to the other side of the block and around to my car, Mister Casual. I didn't know where to start looking for a gun. There were people in Chicago who would have been able to help me, but I didn't know anyone to approach in New York. Kyle would have been my first choice, but Kyle was dead. I could feel a springiness in my arms and legs. I hadn't shot a rifle since summer camp, and had never touched a handgun. Once Burke showed up and realized Nikki didn't have the money, who knew what he might do to her and Alina. What he'd already done. I'd make him drop his gun if he had one and hold him for the cops, like in a movie. I drove out of her neighborhood and called Liz. I got her fucking voicemail again, but she hardly mattered anymore.

I called my cousin Jack down in Houston—who grew up in the house I was now occupying—to see if he might know someone on Long Island who could get me what I needed. We'd been close as kids. I hadn't seen him since my mother's funeral. After he offered condolences for Cynthia, we wandered through the small talk, until I finally asked if he could help me find some coke. There was no point worrying him by mentioning a gun, but the coke might lead to what I needed. Of course it would.

It was the only chance I had. He hemmed and hawed and I told him no, I wasn't planning anything crazy in the wake of Cynthia's death, that I was doing all right, all things considered. Broken up, sure. Devastated, of course. But all right, too. Holding up. It was a delicate balance. I just needed a little something to help with the pain. He told me he'd call back as soon as he determined if anyone was still around.

"But soon," I said. "Right away," I said.

I read his concern through the silence.

"There's this woman," I said.

And I knew I was making it worse. As if I could possibly tell him about Nikki—or even mention her less than a week after Cynthia's death.

"Her sister," I said. "She's fucked up over this whole thing. Like me. But worse. I just thought—"

He told me he'd call back. Soon. Told me to take it easy.

I called Liz again, got her fucking voicemail again.

"Call me back," I said to her voicemail. "If you want me to do this thing with Kara, call me back."

Nikki called and said she'd talked to Alina.

"That's good," I told her. "That's great," I told her.

"I know," she said.

I listened to her cry for a minute.

"That is so great," I told her.

"I know," she said. "I know," she said.

"So," she said, sniffling and crying a little still, "do you have it?"

"Almost," I said. "Just about."

"They're coming at five," she said. "You have to have it."

"I know," I said. "That won't be a problem," I said.

Jack called and I told her I had to go, the money and everything.

"I'll never be able to thank you for this," she said, and I said,

"Yeah, you will," hating myself for saying that, as if she'd owe me, and then I said, "I mean—forget it. I want to do this." And I did.

Jack gave me a name and number.

And I felt this surge.

Burke

We walk on Moses Beach at high tide, not many people out along the water, but the guiding hand of fate everywhere, even in the names of places, *Moses Beach*—like I'm Moses himself, handing down commandments and delivering my brother from his years of suffering and denial, proving again how lined up and right everything is at the moment, though I haven't slept in I don't know how many days and am running out of stories to tell. I ask Alina to tell a story, but she seems tired and fidgety, wrung out from our earlier joy and tears at being reunited.

On the phone at the gas station, Nikki said she'd have the money by five, and I'm wondering if I should just take it and get on my plane for Puerto Rico. Pick up more once I run out. I'm exhausted from Cinnamon and Alina, and I haven't even met Nikki yet. I wonder if I should take Alina with me down to the islands, but that don't seem like much of a vacation, truth be told, and she'll need to be in school, anyway, which makes me wonder why she ain't in school now. I ask her that, why she ain't in school, and she tells me about this asshole Kyle Nikki's been fucking behind my brother's back, how he died last week on a motorcycle—another sign of alignment—with some rich bitch he was fucking behind Nikki's back. Some gigantic soap opera. Alina blubbers about him, how good he was, the best man she's ever known, filling me with so much hatred I can hardly control myself. But at least it wakes me up. And it's another blessing, because now there's no man to jump me, no one to help the whore, more proof of the righteousness of my actions and everything lined up in my favor.

"Is something wrong?" Alina asks.

"What could be wrong?" I say.

Just like her mother, denying Cash, denying me. Running into the arms of some other man ain't never been her real daddy.

"You just seem—"

"Sugar," I say, hugging her by the water. "It breaks my heart to think of everything I missed."

It's not her fault she never knew me. It's that fucking Nikki.

"Can't we go home now?" she says.

"Of course we can," I tell her. "I'm sorry I got quiet like that. Nothing you can do to change the past. What's done is done. You have to live in the present."

"I shouldn't have told you," she says.

"Told me what?" I say, and she says, "About her and Kyle. But she didn't love him. You should know that."

"What about you?" I say. "Did you love him?"

She looks at me with her bottom lip puffed out and trembly.

"I miss him so much," she says.

"But you got me now," I say, trying to tamp down the hatred. "Right?"

I hold her crying against me like that, the waves washing over our bare feet.

"Ain't that just like the guiding hand," I say, "bringing your real daddy back when the fake one's checked out."

"I want to go home," she says. "Can't we go home now?"

"Of course we can," I say, leading her toward the car, thinking maybe I will kill her. Maybe I just will. If my mother was alive, there wouldn't be a question about it. Kill her and take Alina to Waco to be raised up right. Away from Nikki's poison.

She sniffles beside me as we walk the beach. I hand her my bandana to blow her nose into, just like her daddy, not caring

193

about her snot smeared on my handkerchief. But it seems like Puerto Rico might not be the best place to finish raising her. It don't really matter what I decide or don't decide, though. The hand will decide for all of us. I don't want to let my emotions get the better of me—especially my love for Alina, which has been with me nearly all my life, certainly all of hers, from the minute I felt her being born all them years ago at Huntsville. I got to keep my head, even if her lying bitch of a mother does deserve to die. Mostly, I don't want to hurt her more than she's already been hurt. A girl needs her mother. But leaving her with Nikki might just hurt her worse in the long run.

Still, it don't seem right to leave all that money on the table. Kill her now or kill her later, only the hand can decide. You don't want to walk away from money you're owed though, justice always such a tricky thing to figure out.

Alina climbs inside herself on the ride back to Long Beach and Nikki's fate, not talking much, a little ungrateful, really, everything her family's been through, everything I've tried to bring her. It's not her fault, though. Maybe being reunited with her daddy after all this time is too much for her. Maybe the kindest thing would be to put her back with her mama where she belongs. It's like she's pouting, though, something I can hardly tolerate. I know she's tired, but that don't mean she should be ungrateful. And who's the one been up two days without sleep? Who's the one got a right to be tired, all the work I put in? She pouts on the seat beside me till I can hardly stand the silence.

"So you really liked that Kyle," I say, "huh?"

She bursts into tears beside me, her face in her hands, bawling.

I pull to the side of the road and scoot over and hold her as she bawls and shakes against me. Even though she's holding on to me as she cries, I can hardly contain my hatred for that cocksucker Nikki's been fucking behind my back, even if he is dead.

And Alina so ungrateful after everything I done for her, for all of them, everything Nikki's done against us. I don't know what the guiding hand will do with any of us once I see that bitch, but I hope it does decide to kill her. Alina cries and holds on to me, her hands on my back the only thing keeping me from crushing her here and now, her hands on my back even as she denies me with her tears for that asshole, Kyle, and I just don't know how much more denial I can tolerate, praying to the hand she don't become another whore of Babylon like her mother, even if that's what they all become sooner or later. But telling myself, She's your daughter, your daughter, your baby girl, even as she denies and denies and denies me.

31

MARK

I end up in an apartment over a decaying garage in Hempstead with a dirtbag named Stan, figuring I'd better actually buy some blow before mentioning the gun, Stan repeatedly telling me what good people my cousin is as he weighs out an eight ball at the kitchen table.

"Jack ever tell you about the time I ripped off a Dairy Barn," Stan says, "way the fuck out in Shirley?"

I shake my head, but I'm thinking the more criminal Stan is the better.

"You don't want to shit in your own backyard," he says, pouring coke onto a mirror from what must be a two ounce bag. "I'll give you a taste," he says.

I don't want a taste. A taste is the last thing I want. I've only got two hours to get back to Nikki's place, convince her the new plan will work, and hide myself. I don't need to be any more wired than I already am. Or maybe I do.

"We were way the fuck out at Smith Point," he says. "I told Jack that beach ain't shit when you got Jones Beach or Robert Moses so much closer, but he was seeing this skank from East Patchogue, so of course he drags me all the way out there."

He hands me a metal straw. I lower my face and snort a long rail, what seems like a quarter gram.

"You ever been out there?" he says.

I hand him the straw and feel the drip.

"Way out by Moriches? You know—where that plane crashed and everything? It's a cover up, you know, flight 800 or whatever. You know that?"

He does two lines rapidly, one for each nostril, then pops up from the mirror, grinning. "Some good shit, no?"

"Really good," I say.

"My uncle knows this guy," Stan says, "who's out in Moriches Bay that night and seen a cigarette boat launch the missile. Thought it was fireworks—couldn't even see the plane, until it blew up right over him and started raining shit down, body parts and seat cushions and all kinds of shit. Like Hiro-fucking-shima, man. That exactly what he said."

The coke runs through me, cranking me up.

"Hiro-fucking-shima," Stan says, twisting the baggy and tossing it across the table. I hand him the money.

"There's this other thing," I say, "you could maybe help me with," and when he rattles off a list of guns he can probably get and their approximate prices, I want to kiss his dirtbag face. And when I say I need the gun now, like right now, he says he can probably get it in an hour.

"Don't think I do this for anyone," he says. "And it's gonna cost. The piece, plus my time and risk. Let me see what I can do—"

"But I need it now."

"Settle down, bro," he says. "I hear you. Come back in an hour. And tell Jackie to stop by when he's back on the Island. What am I, just criminal element to him now?"

NIKKI

"I need the money now," I tell him.

197

"I'm working on it," he says. "I'll be there in time. But if I'm not, do you have any cash—something to give him while you wait for me?"

I walk to my car, looking all around for somebody watching. Even though I know Burke's probably lying, I can't take any chances. I get the fifteen thousand from the bank and drive home, still seeing no one—time like a sludge I'm wading through. I put the money in a black vinyl bag with a flap and wrap the bundle with twine, focused, knowing I can handle Burke, reaching for the relief that washed over me when I heard Alina's voice on the phone, saying to myself over and over, *She's alive.* I place the money in the crisper drawer of the fridge and call Mark, but he still doesn't have it.

"If you're late," I say, "you're going to have to call. You can't just walk in here. He might think you're a cop. If you're late—"

"I'm not going to be late."

"You can't just walk in here," I say. "That guy—whoever—may be watching."

"I can sneak in the back," he says. "I can leave the money somewhere."

"In the freezer," I say. "But you can't stay here. And you can't let anyone see you or hear you when you come in."

"They didn't see me when I snuck out," he says. "He called after I left, right?"

"Yeah, but—"

"So I can sneak back in."

"But he might—"

"We're going to have to see how it goes. I'm getting the money right now, so I have to go. Okay? But I'll be there in a while. And I'll make sure nobody knows."

If he's late, I don't want him to see what I might have to do.

But I'm so grateful. More than grateful. And maybe he'll understand if something happens and I have to do something. Because I trust him. Maybe I really do trust him. But then I have to move the money, because I'm afraid Burke will kill me when I reach to grab it from the fridge with my back to him.

Thinking, Alina, then pushing it away.

Trying to make myself empty.

I open the bag and look at the money, because I've already scattered everything I can think of as a weapon everywhere.

I can't catch my breath.

The sunlight in the kitchen is too bright and too dull.

Because it's almost time.

Trying not to think she's dead.

That I talked to her and then he killed her.

I'll take her raped and beaten if she's alive. I'll take her any way I can get her.

But if he's hurt her, I'll kill him. That's what I have to contain.

If he hasn't hurt her . . . I'll. . . .

Breathe.

Like labor.

I retie the money bag and drop it in the center of the kitchen table.

I don't know how or where to place myself for their arrival.

And once I get what I want. . . .

I walk to the living room, stick my head out the screen door.

Because I'm stronger than he is.

Walk back to the kitchen.

Because the only thing he has to lose is his miserable, worthless life.

I open a beer and try to drink.

I can't scare Alina. Can't show her more than she's already seen.

And if she honestly believes he's her father. . . .

The beer wants to come back up.

I'll tell her the whole story, not caring anymore what she knows or doesn't know. As long as she's alive.

A car door slams.

I *walk* to the window, but it's just Mrs. Hansen, across the street.

My hands shaking.

He said they'd be here at five.

All of me shaking.

That I was to treat this like a reunion.

The hard part will be making Alina believe. She'll want to see love.

It's four-fifty-two.

But once I know she's okay, I can make myself do anything. Show her whatever she needs to see.

It's been four-fifty-two for an hour.

I realize I'm not dressed for the occasion, panic, and run upstairs to put on my new, black, funeral dress.

When I walk out of my closet, pulling the dress over my head, he's at the door to my room with a gun in his hand, grinning.

My stomach turning inside out.

"Nikki," he says. "We finally meet."

All this ice in me.

"Where's Alina?" I say.

I forget to breathe.

Forget everything.

"Where's Alina?"

"Go on and pull that dress back off," he says. "I think I like you better without it."

MARK

I can only get four hundred from the ATM and Stan wants twelve. I give him the Rolex David Lambert gave me after the '98 recount.

He studies it, considering.

"It's real," I tell him.

He turns it over in his hand.

"Come on, man," I say. "That's worth at least three grand, maybe four. And I'm coming back tomorrow, maybe tonight, with the cash."

"I'll hold the watch," he says, "Until you bring the money. But this ain't a fucking pawn shop."

Nikki seemed better when I talked to her on the phone, more self-contained, but deeper inside herself too, focused on what's in front of her. Maybe too focused, like she could fall all the way into whatever she's becoming and never crawl out.

Stan hands me a nine millimeter pistol with two extra clips in pouches on the band of a shoulder holster, loaded.

He shows me how to pop the clip, how to pull the slide to chamber a round, where the safety is.

"Those are hollow points," he says. "So you can expect a good size hole out the back of whatever you hit."

He wipes the gun with a dishtowel and hands it to me butt first, the towel still wrapped around the barrel in his grip. "Don't do anything stupid with this," he says.

"Okay," I say, but he won't let go.

"I don't care if you're Jack's cousin or not—if this comes back to me. . . ."

"It won't."

"Get your finger away from the trigger," he says. "Even if the safety's on, you don't put your finger near the trigger. Holster it."

I put the gun in the holster, the holster in the grocery bag.

"Don't show it unless you're going to use it," Stan says. "Do you understand? They'll take it away and shoot you. If you show it, you better have the nerve."

He hands me the metal straw and nods toward the mirror on the table. I lean down and snort one line and then another.

"Thanks, man," I say, and Stan says, "God bless."

I chamber a round in the car, but leave the safety on. The gun's heavier than I thought it would be.

"Hit him in the chest," I imagine Kyle saying. "You want a big target."

"The balls," Cynthia says. "Blow his balls off."

I chew the insides of my cheeks as I crawl back down to Long Beach through rush hour traffic. Wondering if I have the nerve.

"You do," Cynthia says. "Of course you do."

"You can do it," Kyle says.

"Take a deep breath before you pull the trigger," Cynthia says. "And hold it."

"Squeeze gently," Kyle says, "as you exhale."

I still hate him. But less.

Maybe I should hate him more, for encouraging me to kill somebody—setting me up for prison.

Not that I plan on killing anyone.

I just need to hold him for the cops.

I cross the bridge over the bay into Long Beach.

"Of course you'll kill him," Cynthia says. "You heard what Stan said. Don't show the gun unless you're going to use it. Do it for her and her kid."

There's a car parked on the street in front of her house.

I drive past, turn the corner and park.

I check the chamber again, but leave the safety on. I'm good at this kind of thing, I remind myself, slinking up the sidewalk toward her house—good at fixing things. But I'm carrying the holstered gun in a grocery bag.

I walk back to the car, dump the bag, unholster the gun, and jam it in my pants like a television killer, hoping I don't blow my own balls off.

Trying to be as strong and focused as Nikki.

"Do it for the baby," Cynthia says. "Do it for everyone."

32

CASH

I didn't know how hurt I was, shock maybe, though the sting where Nikki stabbed me started to rise and radiate as I made my way to the big house on Duval, the seat of my shorts soaked with blood. The place was empty. If I had my mother's gun, I would have gone back and finished it once and for all for the both of us. But I didn't have a gun. I wrapped a bag of ice with a dishtowel and laid against it on the basement couch, chasing Percocets with whiskey until the pain started to back off and I drifted away, Nikki finally floating through the haze and hovering over me like a dream, here and then gone, the fight draining out as we studied each other in the dim light from the stairs.

I told her how much I loved her earlier, when we was making love, told her all the time how much I loved her, did everything I could to prove my love.

What I got in return was a knife in the back.

But she'd had a change of heart and come to me in the fog— her, the one I loved—the two of us watching each other through halos of hate and whiskey and love like ropes around us. Here and then gone. The sting of coming awake. Her worried face looking down on me as I looked up at her as trusting as a newborn baby.

Everything passed between us then, this love we shared, and then the halos had me by the throat, my hand dripping blood down my wrist, leaking from a wound she was ministering to. A halo around my finger. I forgave her everything as she bandaged me up. I knew she finally understood how much I loved her. Even in spite of all my fuck ups, my jealousy and whatnot, me forcing myself on her or whatever it was, I knew how much she loved me, too—how deep our love was for one another, binding us together for here and eternity, me and Nikki, the only one I would ever love.

BURKE

It takes everything I've got not to blow a hole in her standing there by her closet door. She's older, sure, but still nice looking. Maybe not as nice as Cinnamon, but she shows me her lean belly over her panties over her long smooth legs as she pulls that dress over her head like a whore and pretends she didn't hear me coming—doing everything she can to hold me with herself, changing her clothes and showing all that skin, trying to tease me and take me out of my right mind with her whorish way, everything my brother had and should have kept having all them years since the bitch murdered him. And me fighting to keep my head and get what I came for.

When I tell her to go on and pull the dress back over her head to show me what's mine, she acts like she don't hear me. Or that she's the one in charge.

"Where's Alina. Where's Alina." Like a goddamn parrot.

"I told you to take that dress off."

"Where's Alina?"

I walk toward her slow and gentle, then move quick and pop her in the jaw.

"Alina's fine," I tell her.

I can see how hard she's holding herself, wanting to spring

like a cat. Not even touching the spot I popped her, already red and rising.

"Take off your dress," I tell her. "And show me my money."

"Where's Alina?" Anchored to her spot on the floor. But trembling.

"You're shaking, ain't you, Nikki?" I say. "I bet Cash never shook like that."

Looking me in the eye like we're in a staring contest.

"You think I'm going to hurt my own blood?"

Stone faced and rooted to the floor. But that electricity running through her.

"Where's—"

"My own daughter?"

I jerk my hand and she flinches.

"I told you she's fine."

Like a statue shaking, staring at me with all that hate.

"Take off your dress, Nikki. Show me what Cash died for. What Kyle died for."

That gets her a little—Kyle—her lips twitching, but trying to hide it.

"Alina told me about Kyle. I don't think Cash would appreciate that. Do you, Nikki? You fucking old Kyle after killing my brother."

"I need to see Alina," she says. "Then the money."

I hang my head for a second, then slap her in the same spot I popped her before.

She holds herself from fighting back.

I slap her again, but she puts her arms up to cover her face.

I punch her hard in the belly, and she doubles over, her arms around her middle.

I slap her again.

Grab a fistful of hair down by the scalp and pull her up by it. Smack her mouth with my mother's gun. Whap! And get my

205

voice close to her ear, still holding her by her hair. "You do what I say, Nikki, and you'll see Alina. You don't do what I say, and I'll kill you and take her."

I jerk her by the ball of hair in my fist and dump her to the floor. Crouch over her with my knee on her neck.

"I never wanted it to be like this," I tell her.

Her breathing on the floor under my knee.

"You brought this on yourself."

I reach down her body for the bottom of her dress and she starts to wriggle. I put more weight into her neck. Punch her ribs. Hard. "You can take it off or I can take it off," I tell her. I put the gun against her cheek, pushing it into the mess of blood that's running there. "You wanna see Alina?"

She nods, spits out blood.

"You can see her if you want to. It's all up to you."

More nodding, but looking straight ahead, under the bed.

"Is that what you want?"

"Yes."

"That's good. I'm going to lift myself up real gentle. But I don't want you to move. Okay, Nikki? Then when I tell you, I want you to stand up and take off your dress. Then I want you to show me my money. Okay, Nikki? And once we're clear on that, we'll go get Alina and go out for a reunion dinner. And then maybe you and me can pick up where we left off all them years ago, before everything turned to shit. Maybe rediscover our love. Does that sound good, Nikki?"

I raise myself slow with the gun on her.

She doesn't move.

"You can get up now," I say. "I'm sorry I had to hit you, but you have to learn. Go on and pull that dress over your head."

She watches me as she lifts the dress over herself, never taking her eyes from my face.

"I know Cash could be a handful," I say. "I do know that. But you can too, can't you, Nikki. Why don't you turn around and show me yourself."

She turns, but her face is fucked up, half ruined by what she made me do to her. Her ass is good, though, filling her panties, her back smooth and strong. I've got half a mind to take her now, but then realize that's what she wants, the whore, so she can get me in a compromising position and kill me like she killed Cash.

I have to calm myself and keep focused.

Make myself an instrument of the hand.

Her face is all fucked up anyway. Blood smeared. A couple of wobbly front teeth she can't stop running her tongue over.

Hardly worth a man's life now.

"Now you're going to show me the money, Nikki. And then we're gonna get Alina. Doesn't that sound good?"

"It's downstairs," she says. Talking like a zombie.

"Why don't you lead me to it."

She starts for the door and I follow.

"Stop for just a minute and turn around," I tell her.

She turns.

"I'm going to keep this gun on your back, Nikki. If I shoot you—if I kill you, like you killed Cash—you'll never see Alina again. And while that might be fine with me, would have been fine with me, now we have Alina to consider. A girl needs her mama, Nikki."

She stands in front of me, blood running down her neck, speckling her bra. Blood smeared all over her fucked up face.

I heft one of her tits in my hand. Drop it and take the other. Her looking past me. Holding herself tight. Shaking a little. All mine.

And if she makes one move toward me, I'll blow a hole in her.

Her sensing that.

Knowing I want to kill her.

Hoping the hand lets me.

Hoping it keeps her alive for years of payoff.

Payoff and everything growing between us.

Everything she denied Cash. Denied me.

Killing her later. After the payoff.

Trying to make myself an instrument. To surrender to the hand.

"You can take me to the money now," I tell her.

She turns and I follow.

"Why don't you just pull down your panties and show me your ass, Nikki," I say, knowing I can test myself like this, take one look and then get the business done. Prime myself for what will follow, tying her down like she tied Cash and taking something worth more than a finger.

She stands like a statue, then rolls down her panties in front of me, her ass sticking out like a whore's.

"That's good, Nikki," I say. "Now let's get my money."

Trying to hold myself as tight as she is.

NIKKI

I should have hid the money. I should have kept the money hidden until I had Alina safe with me. My only card sitting out on the kitchen table, not that it's enough. Light pouring through the windows all over it. He doesn't know he can't hurt me though. My other card. He doesn't know he can't do anything to me. Except through her.

I walk down the stairs in front of him, my eyes on the potted plant and the kitchen knife. But she could be tied up in a hole somewhere. She could starve to death, tied up in a hole somewhere if I kill him.

My face and head throbbing where he hit me. My broken teeth.

Blood tickling my chest far away under this throbbing of my face, my mouth.

My ass hanging out of my underwear as I walk and him never shutting up. All these words from him. All this noise.

I don't have a single card to play.

Except that he can't hurt me.

I'll kill two brothers, some cunt mother's sons, but maybe she has others.

I'll kill them too.

I stop in the middle of the living room.

"Whoa," he says. "What are we stopping for?"

But not until I know where Alina is.

Grabbing my bare ass and pushing the gun into my back.

"Where's it at?"

"All this blood," I say, smearing my hands and holding them up so he can see.

Waiting for Mark. Because if the money's not enough, he'll kill me and take Alina. If she's—

But if he sees Mark. If he kills Mark and then me. . . .

"I think I'm going to pass out."

Not sure I said it.

"Not now you ain't."

He pushes the gun into my back again.

But I can't kill him now.

"Get me my money."

My hatred a tiny walnut in my chest compressed and contained.

"Aspirin," I say, walking toward the bathroom. "Let me just clean myself up."

"Not until you get my money you ain't."

The gun cracks against my skull.

I fall to the living room floor.

Any delay is good.

Mark will be here with the money, but that's—

He grabs me by my hair again, pulling me up.

I unlock my knees, hanging limp by my hair, the sound of it tearing from my scalp.

Bend and be strong.

He lets go and I drop.

I grunt for him.

He can't hurt me through my body.

The money out on the kitchen table. In broad daylight.

Why he'll never find it.

But not enough.

"I'll drag you by your fucking hair," he says, grabbing and pulling.

And then I think I will pass out.

"No," I say, grabbing at his wrists.

A kind of lightning through my body and eyes as he drops me.

"I'll show you," I say, sitting up.

Because I can't pass out.

He'll take it and kill me and take Alina and kill her.

If she's alive.

I run my hand over the soft spots of my skull. Through the blood on my face. "You know I always loved you," I say. "I never wanted to hurt you. I'm sorry," I say. "I'm sorry!" Crying. "It was an accident! I love you."

"Just shut up," he says. "We can talk about that later. After you show me my money."

I reach back and unclip my bra.

"Oh, no," he says. "It ain't gonna be like that. Not until I see my money."

"The bathroom's right there," I say, dropping my bra to the floor at his feet, and not looking at him.

"Can't I just get cleaned up and take some aspirin? I can't see through this blood."

"Well—"

"I know I was wrong!" I say. "I think about him every day. About you!"

I reach for his leg, not touching it.

I feel his eyes on me. The gun on me.

"I don't want to look like this for you. I don't want to pass out."

He reaches down and takes my breast in his hand, and I put my hand over his, pushing it against me.

His lover. His fucking mother.

I'll kill her too. For bringing him to life. For bringing both of them to life.

And all the others.

"Please?" I say. "Baby? It'll just take a second."

"You think I want to hurt you? Is that what you think?"

"I know you want what's best for me. For Alina."

"You couldn't even give her my name?"

"I'm sorry," I say, bringing my other hand to my face to wipe the tears away. "I know I was wrong. You don't know how much I've hurt for him. For you."

Snot mixing with tears and blood as he keeps palming my tit.

"Please forgive me," I say. "That's all I want. Please. I'll do anything. I'll give anything if you'll forgive me."

"You're just a whore," he says, and I say, "I want us to be together. You and me and Alina."

He takes me by the hair again, and I lift myself under his pulling hand, the gun jamming against what must be a broken rib, sending flashes of light across my vision.

"Get cleaned up, Nikki," he says. "But we ain't making love till you show me my money."

"Okay," I say, trying to see through the lightning. "Whatever you want, Daddy."

"Killer. Liar. Whore," he says. "Don't think I'll forget."

"But if you could teach me—"

"Shut up."

He slaps me, but I don't fall to the floor this time, hanging my head instead, meek, beaten. His beaten little doll. Stronger every time he hits me.

Not knowing what I'm supposed to do. Because if the money's not enough and he kills me, and then Alina will—

"Clean your face," he says, pushing me toward the bathroom. "Take your pills."

I run water in the sink, him in the mirror behind my back over my bloody face, pushing himself against me. I need to stop time here.

"Maybe you can learn," he says. "Maybe be forgiven."

I need time to stop.

"It ain't up to me, though. It's all the hand."

"But she's okay, right?"

"Goddammit," he says grabbing my hair again. "Why you always got to talk about her?"

"I—"

"You never loved me."

"No. I do. I love you!"

He yanks me by the hair and turns me, pushing me out of the bathroom, the gun against my back.

"Get me my money right now," he says. "It's not even up to me. None of it is. You brought this on yourself. Just do it. Or I swear to god I will kill you here and now."

And I believe him and won't be able to do a thing, won't be able to find her if he kills me, and I say, "The kitchen," leading him there by my hair in his hand. "But Alina—"

"Shut up about Alina, you goddamn—always bringing her between us. She's already dead! Okay? Just like Cash. Just like you. I told you that! My own fucking blood. Everything you've done. She's dead!"

I can hardly see through the blood and lightning and knowing what I knew all along, Alina, but no, Alina, but *no*, knowing what I knew but not knowing and knowing what I knew, *Alina*. I hear a thump and him falling and Mark's there with a gun and a hammer as I spin around, Burke on the floor, holding his head and thrashing. I reach for Mark's gun, for Mark's arm holding the gun, directing it at the fucking fucking fucking fucking fucking fucking, saying through my broken mouth, in my head, through my whole body, "Shoot him. Kill him! Give me that. Kill him. Let me have it," Mark getting an arm around me and pulling me in, the gun still pointing at Burke on the floor, Mark trying to contain me, saying, "No. Nikki. Stop. I've got it. Just stop. I've got it. Stop."

But I cannot stop.

Alina.

Fuck.

Alina.

Fuck

Noises coming out of me as I thrash for the gun. Because there's no reason not to kill him now, all of it erupting out of me, Mark screaming in my ear around the noises coming from inside as he keeps trying to pull me in: "No, Nikki. Stop. Stop!"

But I will never be able to stop.

MARK

I see them in the living room through the screen door, him with a gun on her pushing her toward the bathroom. Blood runs down her beat up face and over her breasts, the left side of her face like raw meat, bruised and bloody and swollen. He pushes her toward the bathroom, telling her to take her pills, and I run around the side of the house under the bathroom window—him above me telling her she can maybe be forgiven—to the back door, closing it silently as I ease into the house, shaking and trying to get up my nerve, knowing I can kill him after what I've seen. But still shaking.

I hide myself against the kitchen wall by the entrance to the living room.

A slamming from the bathroom.

I look at the gun in my hand shaking.

The safety's still on.

I push it off, the red dot showing.

There's a hammer on the counter.

"You never loved me!" he screams.

Maybe killing her.

I poke my head around the entryway, and he's pushing her out of the bathroom toward me, holding her by her hair in his fist. The big hole Stan told me about if I shoot him once he walks past me, the bullet going into her.

I pull my head in fast, waiting for them coming toward me.

The noise and the feeling of them through the floor. Her stumbling and asking about Alina and him saying she's already dead as he pushes her past me.

Already dead!

He's got her hair in his fist as he walks past.

Nikki starts wailing.

But if I shoot him now I might kill them both, the bullet going through him and into her. Or he might get a shot off into her back.

"My own fucking blood!" he screams, as she thrashes against him.

He wraps her in his arms, his gun pointed at the wall.

I pick up the hammer and bring it down at the base of his skull, Nikki thrashing and wailing.

He crumples. Nikki whirls, blood-covered, grabbing my arm, going for the gun. My arm part of the gun. I drop the hammer.

214

Burke writhes on the floor holding his head.

Nikki thrashing in my grip, screaming, "Kill him! Kill him!"

I try to keep my eyes on him as I hold her thrashing, try to keep her from killing him. Because I've got him.

I see his gun by the back door as she thrashes against me and he writhes on the floor, screaming. "You fucking fuck!"

Nikki like an animal, twisting out of my hold.

No reason to kill him now, except I want to.

"What do *you* want?" he says bringing himself to his knees.

But it would be better to let the cops have him.

"Who are you?" he screams.

Even though they'll fuck everything up.

"Don't move," I tell him, holding the gun in front of me.

"I'll fucking kill you," he says.

Nikki lifts a chair in the air as if she's going to smash him with it.

But I can't have her so close to him, can't have her take his bullet.

She brings the chair down hard on top of him.

I move quick and push her toward the back door.

"Get out of the way!" I shout.

Blood running down his face now too.

This crazy high pitched screaming from Nikki. This keening.

Him not knowing where to look, at me or at Nikki.

"Don't fucking move!" I scream over Nikki's sounds.

Then she's right above him with his gun in her hand.

"No, Nikki! I say.

But she's got him by the hair, standing behind him.

"No," I say.

He turns to her. Looks up at her.

Grabs her wrist holding his hair.

I shoot him in the chest and he collapses.

Nikki still holding his head by his hair.

With her other hand, she puts the gun against the side of his face and fires.

He jerks down to the floor, a hole in his head.

A hole in his chest.

She stands over him.

"Don't," I say.

She bends over him and fires into the side of his face. Four more times.

Smoke in the kitchen. This stink. Nikki still wailing, keening.

Sounds I've never heard a human make.

I drop the gun on the table and grab her.

She gets off one more shot into his body, keeps pulling the trigger, thrashing in my hold, the sound of clicks on empty chambers under her animal noise, the stink and smoke all around us as she thrashes. I wrap her in both my arms and pull her into me. As hard as I can, hurting her, trying to push her back into herself. Burke running all over the floor.

Another sound. Another screaming.

She must hear it too, because she goes softer in my arms.

Her head perking toward the sound.

She goes silent.

And it's just the other sound.

Alina in the living room at the entrance to the kitchen wailing.

33

ALINA

"Alina," my mother says, and he lets her go.

"Alina!" my mother screams. If it is my mother. This monster. This bloody animal. "Oh, my God. Alina." Stumbling over him toward me. "Baby, baby, baby."

Coming at me naked and bloody.

"Don't look, baby. It's not what you think."

I saw her kill him.

He told me to wait at the diner, where he left me.

I saw her kill him!

But I couldn't wait anymore.

"Look at me, Alina," she says, practically tackling me in the living room as I run. "Oh, baby." Pulling me against her bloody body.

I try to twist out of her hold.

My father!

The words echoing in my dull ears after the explosions and the roaring ringing that won't go away.

"Look at me," she says, turning me into her and holding me away.

"He did this to me," she says, her words jumbled.

Her teeth broken out of her bloody face.

"He's not your father," she says. "He did this to me."

I can't look at her.

"Alina."

But I won't look.

"Alina!"

My legs running, but her holding me.

"He was going to hurt you," she says. "Look at me, baby. It's okay, now. He's not your father. Everything he told you—"

"We have to get out of here," the other one says. Radiant and shiny.

"There might be somebody else," he says, "out there waiting."

"Baby," she says, running her hands over my hair as I twist away.

I throw up all over her as she holds me twisting.

The man appears with her robe from upstairs. A brown bag in his other hand.

Sounds come from me. This shrieking in her face.

"We're going to get you somewhere safe," the man says. "We need to move now."

"Baby," she says, pulling me against her broken body. "I thought you were dead."

Like I thought my father was dead. Back before he wasn't dead.

Back before she didn't kill him.

"He's not your father," she says.

Smearing me with her blood and his blood as I wriggle away.

The man surrounding us with himself, squeezing.

"Stop," he says. "Shh," he says.

"My ribs," she says.

"Alina," the man says, still holding me as he lowers her to the floor.

He lifts me in the air and my legs keep running.

"It's okay," he says. "Alina. It's okay."

I look at my mother dead on the floor.

My father dead in the kitchen.

He tried to kill her. And then she killed him.

I call her name as loud as I can. I call her name.

"She's going to be okay," the man says. "She's going to—Shh. We're going to get her somewhere safe. We're going to get you somewhere safe. Shh. It's okay now, Alina. You're going to help me help your mother. We're going to help her now."

Squeezing the breath out of me as I call her name.

He sets me beside her. "I want to make sure she's okay. I want to show you."

Her not moving all bloody on the floor.

"Mom?" I say.

And I think no and I think no and I think no.

"Heart's beating strong," he says, taking my hand and pushing it against the sticky pulse in her neck. "See? We need to get out of here now. In case—"

"Mom?"

Her eyelids fluttering until she sees me.

She smiles and dies again.

"I'm going to pull the car up front," the man says. "We have to go."

"Mom?"

She wakes again and looks at me.

"It's okay," she says. But her face twists under her mask as she tries to lift herself.

"Just lay still," I say. "Just—"

A hand on my back scares me out of my skin and I shriek.

"It's okay, Alina" the man says.

"It's not okay," I say.

"We just have to get through these next few minutes," he says.

He crouches next to her, lifts her from the floor.

I follow him out the door, closing it behind me.

Mrs. Hansen watches from her porch across the street talking into her phone, one hand saluted on her forehead against the setting sun.

The man waves me to the open back car door.

"Sit with her head in your lap," he says.

I scoot in as he lifts her head and lays it on my lap.

"Mom?" I say. I can hear her breath bubbling as he pulls away from the curb.

"I think she's dying," I say, because of that bubbling choking noise.

"Lift her head so she can breathe," the man says.

I try not to hurt her as I lift her head higher and she coughs.

"Mom?" I say.

The man hands me a wet towel over the front seat as we cross the bridge.

I try to touch her face with it, to clean up the blood.

"I thought you were dead," she says, looking up at me.

"Alina," she says. "*Alina.*"

"If that wasn't my father. . . ."

"His brother," she says. "Burke."

She grimaces as I smear blood on her face.

"I'm sorry," I say. "I'm sorry," I say.

"It's okay," she says, but her words are smashed. "I'm just so happy."

"But Mom? But Mom?"

She opens her eyes.

"Where are we going?"

"The cops," the man says, and my mother says, "No!" and the man says, "I really think," and my mom says, "Later!"

"The hospital then," the man says.

"But not the cops, Mark. Not yet. Not the hospital, either. I'm not ready."

"Listen," he says, and my mother says, "Not like this. No! I have to get cleaned up. I'm not going like this."

The man doesn't say anything. "Promise me," she says, and he still doesn't say anything, and she says, "Promise me, Mark," and he says, "Okay. Shh."

And then she's asleep, the towel against her face under my hand under her hands.

"Mom?"

She opens her eyes and closes them.

"Mom?"

She opens her eyes and closes them.

"Where are we going?"

"I know a place we can rest," Mark says, "that's safe."

"But what about the hospital," I say. "That's where we need to go."

"I know" Mark says. "And we will. Soon."

"But what if she's dying."

"I'm not dying," she says. "I wouldn't be able to say this if I was."

"But what if you are?"

"Shh," she says, looking into my face. Falling asleep, then saying my name.

"Stay awake," I tell her. "I think it's bad if you go to sleep."

"Alina," she says, looking up at me. "I'm resting."

I hold her.

"Lina," she says. "My beauty."

The man drives us past the airport, planes rising and falling, and toward the city into the sun going down.

34

MARK

I need to get her to the hospital and we need to talk to the cops, but I'm not even sure what to tell the cops. I don't know anything, but I feel okay for the moment. I mention the hospital again as we walk up the stairs to Cynthia's apartment, and Nikki says she has to get cleaned up first, that she won't go anywhere looking like this. I don't know if the emergency room will be legally compelled to notify the cops. Nikki has her arm around Alina, glowing through the mess Burke made of her. She seems to be feeling better since her rest in the car. I grab Cynthia's camera from her bedroom closet and tell Nikki I have to take some pictures of her if we aren't going to the cops right away.

"It would be better if we went now," I tell her. "We need to show them what he did to you," but she shakes her head.

I know we need to tell them something and soon, even if we don't turn ourselves in right away. And time will help me get us help with our approach. But every second of silence smears us with guilt. If only she hadn't shot him. It would be so much better if there was only the one shot, my shot, if it had only been me that killed him. Then they could just disappear into the world somewhere. Even if it was just one shot from her. But unloading the gun like she did, I just don't know how that will play, and everything buried back in Texas that will have to come out, these dead brothers, even if they deserved it and none of it was her fault. But it should have been only me that shot him, like I wanted it to be.

I get her some Vicodins from Cynthia's medicine cabinet.

Nikki stands in Cynthia's bikini in Cynthia's living room, euphoric, while I take pictures of her beat up body and face. Her ribs where he kicked her are bruised bad and bloody.

"He was sick," she tells Alina, who's slouched into Cynthia's couch.

The cat people upstairs drag a pallet of concrete across their floor.

"It seemed so true," Alina says. "He had pictures of him and you."

"But that would have been Cash," Nikki says. "Not Burke."

"Cash," Alina says. "My father."

"Yes."

"Did you love him?"

"I was very young."

"Did you?"

"Yes. And I always loved you."

I feel like I should leave them alone, but calling attention to myself with movement seems like an interruption.

"He said you wanted an abortion, that he talked you out of it."

"That's not true, Alina. And that wasn't even him. Remember? I never even met Burke. He was in prison then."

"He said he talked you out of it."

I try to make myself invisible.

"But that wasn't your father. And I never had that thought. Not even once. I always wanted you."

I'm so tired now and don't know what to do exactly, wishing I could just get them out of here and away somewhere safe forever.

She sits with Alina on Cynthia's couch, petting her, both of them covered with dried, cracking blood. Everything quiet a minute. Then Nikki says, "Let's take a bath," rising from the couch and holding a hand out to Alina.

I run the water for them, get them towels.

I check my voicemail while they're in the tub together, three calls from Liz, all too late. But it would have been too late no matter when she called. I never would have gotten that money in time. And the money wouldn't have mattered. If only she hadn't shot him—but maybe I can say I did it. Alina though. Piling lies on her to carry the rest of her life. I call Liz and tell her I need the best lawyer in New York, a politically connected criminal defense attorney. I tell her everything.

"So you killed him?" she asks.

"I don't know."

"But you shot him. First."

"Yes."

"Let me go through the New York House delegation and figure out who to approach."

I tell her I need two attorneys with deep Nassau County political connections, one for me and one for Nikki, and that we'll need to get *Newsday* involved somehow.

She says she gets it. She says she knows.

"And I'll take care of the business with Kara," I tell her. "I'll take care of everything."

"We're not talking about that now," she says. "We're not even thinking about it."

She tells me she'll figure out the lawyers we'll need in New York and Texas, and that she'll study the political machines to figure out where the grease will need to be applied. She'll take care of everything that needs to be taken care of out in the world, while I take care of Nikki and Alina.

That's all I have to do right now.

"Think you can handle that?" she asks me. "While I do this other stuff?"

I think I can handle it, I tell her. I hope I can handle it, I tell her.

"You can handle it," she tells me. "I know you can."

"I don't know how to thank you," I say, because I've never felt such gratitude in my life. Not for the lawyers, or how she'll gear up the apparatus—I'll be paying for all of that in a variety of ways—but just that there's someone working for us, someone I can trust who can actually help us, who knows what I'm supposed to do, too.

"You've never known how to thank anybody," Liz says. "Just do your job and I'll do mine," and I say, "Thank you, Liz," but she's already gone, already working her phone, probably, buying us breathing space for the next few hours and days as she organizes the people who will become our advocates. And whatever I have to pay for that, I will gladly pay.

NIKKI

Alina sits between us in the front seat as we drive to the hospital. I promised her in the tub I'd go to the cops, but I don't know if I'll be able to keep that promise. I want to keep it, but the cops have never done a thing for me and I've done all right without them. If I do go, Mark and I will have to figure out where to put her. I know they're going to lock me up, but if there's somewhere safe to put her, and if that's what she wants—

"Just drop me out front," I tell Mark, as we approach the hospital. "You can pick me up after, if you don't mind."

"No!" Alina says. "I want to go with you!"

"I might be here all night, baby. I want you to sleep."

"No!" Alina says. "We should stay together!"

I pull her into me and look at Mark, his eyebrows raised in a question, like, *Why can't we come with you?*

I shake my head. I still don't know how it will play, and I can't have her talking in there, saying too much. "I need you to take care of her," I say to Mark.

"No!" Alina says, burrowing against my broken ribs.

I grit my teeth to keep from flinching.

"It's okay," Mark says, rubbing his hands up and down her back, still looking at me, evaluating me.

"It's okay, baby," I say. "Do you think I would ever leave you?"

"I don't know," she says, and Mark says to me, "You might like to have us there with you," and I give him a look, like, *Please just do this for me*, and he says, "We'll pick up your mom in a little while, Alina."

I don't want her to be dragged through something else—I know how they'll treat me in there, and I don't want her to see that, to identify as the fucked up kid of the beat up mom. I just need to get through this. Alone. I just need to go inside that machine and come back out, like I have before, and I don't want her to see that. And if we do have to run, I need her safe and ready and not saying too much.

"Baby," I say, "we can talk on the phone if you want, while I wait—the whole time, if you want. Or you can just chill for a while. And the minute I'm ready to go, you'll come get me with Mark. You two can eat something and watch a movie. You don't want to go in there. There's all kinds of gross stuff in there, diarrhea all over the place and people throwing up and screaming and bleeding, and just—"

"Okay," she says. "But you'll call when you're ready."

"Of course I will."

I pet her and kiss her and smell her and kiss her and transfer her to Mark, then walk inside for my long wait with the bleeders.

"I fell," I tell the nurses, a doctor, whoever asks.

They try to make me tell the truth, but give up pretty quickly. They clean my wounds and tape my ribs and leave me for the oral surgeon, who tells me he's going to sew me up and reset bones and pull the teeth that are goners. I can see a dentist in the morning, but I'll leave tonight with a lot of teeth missing.

All the time wondering what to do with Alina. She wants me to go to the cops, and it almost seems like I should. I can't run with her, hiding her, especially after everything I told her in the tub, everything about my past and how she came to be. She took it all much better than I thought she would, but she's in shock, of course, everything she's seen. I can't hide anything from her now. Burke's family might still be alive in Texas, might try to claim her, but maybe after what he's done, the cops will see that they're the unfit ones, not me. I didn't start any of it and was just protecting my baby. Anyone could see that. Mark's getting lawyers set up, and I don't let myself hope for anything with him, even if it does feel like we're all together, and maybe, maybe, but I can't let myself look into the future at all, because that never works, just that we're together now, and *Alina*.

The doctors and nurses treat me like an animal, another fucked up woman from the street. They're not cruel. Just clinical. Indifferent. Mark never asked for anything in return. Him and Alina and the promise I made. I'll take him and You can take me, but You didn't take me. I'll tell them I shot him if that's what Alina wants. It's what she knows. What she saw. What's true. Part of what's true. She's going to need somebody to help her with that, everything she's seen and what she thought she knew, everything she didn't know. Mark will help. I know that now. Mark will help. And her back there waiting for me, alive.

35

BURKE

My Alina—the truest thing that ever happened to me. My baby. How I always knew her. How I felt her being born all those years ago at Huntsville. How I'll always have her. My Alina. Me and Cash and Cinnamon and Nikki and me and my mother and Alina. All my dreams of Nikki and me coming truer and truer, falling in love like the movies you see, where it's him and her and they can't get enough, and it ain't gonna end and it ain't gonna wear off, me and Nikki and Cinnamon forever and Alina.

ALINA

Mark puts me in her bed and sits on the edge reading to me like I'm a kid. I cried after we dropped her off. I couldn't stop crying and shaking. Mark brought me back upstairs to Cynthia's house and put ice cream in front of me. I can't stop seeing a corner of it. I don't want to look, but a corner of it's at the side of my vision, her over him shooting. The way he flopped. Her noises, these piercing screeches like awful tortured birds. The sound of her shooting again and again. All the sounds. Only sounds. Because everything else is hidden at the corners.

I felt better to be with her when she wasn't dead and I thought she was and then she wasn't and then she told me everything in the bath together. But now she's gone and I don't know if I'll see her again. I don't want to live in Cynthia's apartment. I want to go home.

But I can't go home because that's where everything happened and he's there.

"What if she just gets up and leaves?" I ask him. "After they fix her. What if she just leaves," but even saying that, I know it's not true, and Mark says, "She won't leave. She'll call us and we'll pick her up."

"Are they going to put her in jail?"

"I don't know," Mark says. "But whatever happens, we're going to have good people helping us, people who understand that your mom was just trying to protect you."

"Where will I go? If she goes to jail?"

I don't want to wander between foster families alone while she's in jail, but maybe Ashley's mom will take me. Or maybe after she knows what happened she won't want to take me. Maybe nobody will. Maybe I can live by myself somewhere until she gets out.

I listen to the sound of his voice, but not what he says, as I drift off, and then he's carrying me down the stairs like he carried her before, like she carried me when I was little, but I don't act like I'm awake or anything. I let him carry me to the car and to her, my body loose like I practically am asleep, trying to keep it that way, trying not to be afraid, trying not to see anything at the corners.

MARK

I finally put Nikki with Alina in Cynthia's bed and take the living room couch, falling into a dream of Cynthia and me on a horse riding through trees, all these branches whipping our faces, my arms around her waist and feeling her ribs as she looks back at me smiling. We tumble through space still attached to the horse, meteors shooting around us, and she keeps up that soothing smile before turning into my mother and then Nikki, or maybe she's been Nikki all along, and then she's herself again, smiling, and we're so glad to see each other, so glad to be near each other. I run my hands under her shirt, over the smooth, warm skin of her belly, where I've always put my hands before, and then we're flying, not in planes, but soaring over various incredible pieces of the earth in our bodies. "We're getting out," she says. "We're going away. Finally."

"This isn't possible," I say, even as we fly over farms and cities and deserts and oceans and, finally, above the geometry of the landscape, into black space.

"It is for me," she says.

"That's because you're dead," I say.

She smiles back at me. "Look how we're flying," she says.

"It's just a dream," I say. "It doesn't mean anything."

She doesn't care. I don't care either.

I wake and it's silent in the apartment. Even the cat people upstairs are at rest. The dream lingers. I don't know what's going to happen to me or to any of us. I think about Alina and Cynthia's baby. About Nikki.

She looked awful when we picked her up, her face horribly swollen under the gauze and stitches, her mouth all fucked up. We talked for a while after Alina fell asleep. I told her about my sisters, who I knew would look after Alina if Nikki had to do time. I told her about Lambert and Kara Tomlinson.

"So you have something on him," she said, "this political asshole. That's why I get a big shot lawyer?"

"That's one way to look at it," I said. "Or—I'm helping him. Now he's going to help me. You."

"They'll bring in other people," Nikki said. "From the state. CPS. Everything back in Texas. I go to prison and what happens to Alina?"

"You don't know you're going to prison. And, anyway, that's why I told you about my sisters. People who can step in to help."

"Why can't you do it?" she said.

I walked to the kitchen counter.

"Why can't you take her?" she said. "Until I come back."

I poured more wine in my glass.

"I would take her," I said, surprised that it was true. I hardly even knew Alina.

But, yes, I thought, I'd take her. And we'd wait for Nikki.

It would have to be only about Alina. But I'd take her. That wouldn't happen, though, because I was going to have my own legal problems.

"I would take her," I said again. "But I'm going to have my own situation."

"Because you helped me?" she said.

"We'll have to talk to the lawyers," I said.

"We'll tell them you weren't even there."

"Let's just tell them what happened," I said.

"We should just take off," she said.

It sounded fantastic—running together.

"But I'm done with all that," she said.

"Right," I said.

"For Alina," she said.

"We should go to bed," I said, and she said, "I don't want to close my eyes. I don't want to think about it or replay it. I don't believe any of that therapy shit about facing your problems to put them behind you. I believe in outrunning them."

I looked at her smiling at me with her broken mouth.

"Come sit with me on this shitty couch," she said. "Would you?"

I sat beside her.

"I want this night to last just a little longer."

"Because it was such a great night?"

"Because she's alive. We're all here alive. For just a minute more."

She leaned into me and I wrapped my arm around her listening hard for her breathing, wanting to put my hand on her chest to feel her heart beating, on her neck again, on her wrists, all the places I could feel her pulse, the two of us here right now forever, the three of us, her and me and Alina asleep in the other room fine.

NIKKI

I keep nodding off against him, the fog of drugs lingering over the pain in my body, my face and ribs and mouth, everywhere. Alina asleep in the bedroom. Burke gone where he belongs. Mark never asking for anything. I don't want to be careful anymore. I don't want to run and hide and be careful always for the rest of my life. I don't know why he's here, but I know I'd be dead if he wasn't. Alina with Burke. Everything gone if it wasn't for him. Here beside me.

"She was in love with him," I say. "Cynthia. With Kyle."

"Yeah. Now they're together."

"That's the only way? Dead?"

"Together forever."

"I don't believe that. But he was in love with her, too. He didn't know how deep their connection was."

"They're gone now."

"Let me have some of that wine."

I lift myself from his shoulder and he walks to the kitchen and pours me a glass, and another for himself. Whatever happens now, she's alive and I'm alive. Mark here, too, with us. He brings me wine, and I fight the fog of drugs over the pain in my body, light now, almost floating. Everything we could have lost and didn't.

He lowers himself into the couch beside me floating.

I don't feel like I'm waiting for anything.

I just want this night to last a little longer.

Acknowledgments

I'm grateful to the people who helped me imagine and reimagine this book—Joseph Salvatore, Jess Walter, Jane Ligon, Shawn Vestal, Paul Mandabach, Ellen Schuler Mauk, Robert Lopez, Lynn Trenning, Ken Collins, Brian Mandabach, and Kate Lebo. Thank you.

Author

Photo by Heather Malcolm

Samuel Ligon is the author of a novel, *Safe in Heaven Dead*, and two collections of stories, *Wonderland*, illustrated by Stephen Knezovich, and *Drift and Swerve*. He teaches at Eastern Washington University in Spokane, and is the editor of *Willow Springs*.

Links

Visit Leapfrog Press on Facebook
Google: Facebook Leapfrog Press
or enter:
https://www.facebook.com/pages/Leapfrog-Press/222784181103418

Leapfrog Press Website
www.leapfrogpress.com

About the Type

This book was set in Minion Pro. Minion is an Adobe Originals type-face designed by Robert Slimbach. It was inspired by classical, old style typefaces of the late Renaissance, a period of elegant, beautiful, and highly readable type designs. Minion Pro exhibits the aesthetic and functional qualities that make text type highly readable.

Designed by John Taylor-Convery
Composed at JTC Imagineering, Santa Maria, CA